My God. My God. They are all gone. The
they committed against each other and t

MW00716108

Systema Paradoxa

Accounts of cryptozoological import

Volume 13
Hell's Well
A Tale of The Lone Pine Mountain Devil

As accounted by Sean Patrick Hazlett

NeoParadoxa
Pennsville, NJ
2022

PUBLISHED BY
NeoParadoxa
A division of eSpec Books
PO Box 242
Pennsville, NJ 08070
www.especbooks.com

ISBN: 978-1-949691-81-8
ISBN (ebook): 978-1-949691-80-1

Interior Design: Danielle McPhail
www.sidhenadaire.com

Cover Art: Jason Whitley
Cover Design: Mike and Danielle McPhail, McP Digital Graphics
Interior Illustration: Jason Whitley

Copyediting: Greg Schauer and John L. French

DEDICATION

T his story is dedicated to the person who inspired it, my daughter Erika. Back in 2015, as a Scholastic Kid Reporter, she had the opportunity to interview theoretical physicist Dr. Kip Thorne and British-American screenwriter Jonathan Nolan at NASA's Jet Propulsion Laboratory in Pasadena, California. She asked them questions ranging from Hollywood screenwriting to spinning black holes and time dilation to controversial theories involving wormholes and time travel. Two years later, Dr. Thorne and several of his colleagues won the Nobel Prize for his contributions to the Laser Interferometer Gravitational Wave Observatory (LIGO) detector and the observation of gravitational waves. After the interview, Dr. Thorne wrote the following message to my daughter: "I want you to know that Jonathan Nolan and I both think that your questions at the Interstellar press conference today were by far the best questions anybody asked. You are very impressive." As a father, I could not have been prouder of her.

CHAPTER ONE

THE CRYPTID HUNTER

Dr. Kate Gavin Weaver was one of the few people on the planet who could detect the point source of a gravitational wave within half a parsec, but she still couldn't get her child to eat her corn flakes. Veronica sat at the kitchen table playing with a green plastic allosaurus, humming the CNN jingle as it played on the small television hanging on the wall. In between twirling her pigtails, Veronica scooped up her cereal slower than a tortoise on heroin crawling through a vat of molasses.

Kate tapped her foot impatiently. "Hurry up, honey, and finish your breakfast. You're gonna be late for school."

"But Willy still wants to play," Veronica said in her squeaky four-year-old voice.

"You can play with your dinosaur later. Finish your cereal now. We need to go."

"Okay, Mommy," Veronica said as she continued to do everything but eat her cereal.

Kate was going to be late for work again. Normally, she could get away with it. Aside from her classes, she had a fairly flexible schedule. But today, of all days, being early was existential. Today had been years in the making. It would finally put Kate on the map in the elite astrophysics community. She'd spent years developing a more precise method to filter faint gravitational wave anomalies from the universe's cosmic noise. Her technique leveraged the gravitational emissions of binary neutron stars to triangulate these perturbations in space-time. Her innovation would enable astrophysicists to predict the formation of black holes and other phenomena. Her work was of such promise, it had attracted the notice of Nobel Laureates like Trip Dorn, who now actively collaborated with Kate on much of her research.

Raising Veronica as a single mother and fighting for tenure at one of the world's premier scientific institutions made for an exhausting existence, but Kate had no choice. She'd put herself on this path, and, by God, she'd finish it. She was so close to realizing her lifelong ambition of becoming a Full Professor of Theoretical Astrophysics at Caltech.

Today was supposed to be the big payoff — the first time in her career she'd present her research to the general public as part of the Earnest C. Watson Lecture Series. The program, founded in 1922, showcased the pioneering work of Caltech faculty to a lay audience. While conducting cutting-edge research was a necessary criterion for securing tenure, it was not sufficient. Caltech faculty had to have a rock-star attraction that transcended the incestuous confines of the academy. The ability to articulate esoteric research in simple terms so it was readily accessible to the broadest possible audience was a clear indicator of this quality.

The toaster dinged. Kate grabbed her toast and hastily smothered it with margarine. She glanced up at the television. When she saw her father's face, she grimaced, then turned up the volume.

CNN correspondent, metrosexual Harrison Robbins, stood in front of her grandparents' home in Aston, Pennsylvania. An image of her father, Mack Gavin, dominated the screen's right panel.

"No single media personality has done more to transform the art of the documentary than Dr. Mack W. Gavin," the hoary-haired and bespectacled Robbins said in a confident and self-aggrandizing tone. "Better known by his moniker, The Cryptid Hunter, Gavin has enthralled and entertained audiences for nearly a decade with his hard-hitting and scientifically robust cryptid documentaries. The celebrated cryptozoologist single-handedly legitimized a field of scientific inquiry that had been traditionally relegated to an intellectual backwater, and, if I were to be even less charitable, the province of quackery and pseudoscience."

Kate rolled her eyes. "Well, you should be less charitable, because it *is* pseudoscience," she mumbled.

"Mommy, why is Pop-Pop on TV?" Veronica asked.

"Hush, honey. I'm trying to listen to this."

Robbins continued, "Mack catapulted to fame with an intense docuseries he did on the Dark Watchers of Big Sur. Though the findings of that docuseries were inconclusive, the show launched his Hollywood career and led to ten six-episode seasons of *The Cryptid Hunter*. The sixtieth episode on the Lone Pine Mountain Devil was planned to commemorate the series' ten-year anniversary."

"What a joke," Kate muttered. "If I don't make tenure, it'll be because of that dope."

B-roll footage of Mack replaced his static image as Robbins continued his fawning monologue. "Gavin is not without controversy. His enthusiastic and over-the-top, death-defying bravado can be infectious, but his plain-spoken manner and foul language can be off-putting to more family-oriented audiences. Like any celebrity, Gavin is a complicated man with his own unique faults and foibles, but most adore him."

Kate stuck a finger in her mouth and made a retching sound.

Dr. Chip DeWalt Tuttle appeared in the right panel.

"You have got to be fucking kidding me," Kate said, then belatedly covered her mouth.

"Ewww, Mommy said a bad word," Veronica said.

"I'm sorry, honey. Don't ever repeat it." Kate blushed.

"Chip, over this past decade, you've come to know and respect Dr. Gavin," Robbins said, "what impressed you most about him?"

"I don't have time for this," Kate said as she raised the remote to turn off the television.

"Before Mack's disappearance," Tuttle answered, "I really treasured..."

"Wait. What?" Kate said. She lowered the remote, listening intently as Tuttle completed his sentence.

"…our weekly chats. The man was a force of nature. When he really believed in something, he went the extra mile to make sure his facts were tight. Unassailable. I really hope the authorities are able to locate him."

"Thanks, Chip," Robbins said.

The sketch of a dinosaur-like creature replaced Chip's image.

Veronica pointed at the TV. "Look, Mommy, a dinosaur! Isn't he cute?"

"For folks just tuning in," Robbins said, "Dr. Mack Gavin, the Cryptid Hunter, has been missing for a week. He was last seen in Lone Pine, California doing prep work for the tenth-year anniversary episode of the award-winning *The Cryptid Hunter* series. Studio execs say he was researching the region's Mountain Devil. By all accounts, the episode was to be the capstone event of Gavin's storied career."

Kate's eyes were now transfixed by the television. She stopped breathing, anxious to hear more. Time became meaningless. Almost immediately, a lump of guilt lodged in her throat. All those years of resenting his success came crashing down on her. Now, all she felt was angst and regret.

"What is the Lone Pine Mountain Devil?" Robbins asked. "Unfortunately, Gavin never had the opportunity to answer that question, but I'm confident that if he had, he'd have settled the matter for all time. Some experts have suggested this cryptid could be a missing link to the dinosaurs, much like the Komodo dragon or alligator."

Kate hadn't spoken to her father in a year. In her view, his high-profile reputation as a borderline conspiracy theorist had made her path to tenure much more difficult, and a series of confrontations between them had led to their estrangement. Kate's divorce three years ago had also been a constant source of tension between the two. The divorce was a deep wound for Kate that she felt her father had never shied away from poking.1} But in the face of her father's disappearance, all of it seemed petty to her now. His eyes welled up, then she looked at Veronica and turned away. Kate couldn't let her daughter see her like this. Not now, when she needed to show her strength.

The obese face of a man with flowing, curly red hair and matching neck-beard materialized on the screen's right panel, replacing the Lone Pine Mountain Devil sketch.

"With me today is Sebastian Sanford, Director of the North American Cryptozoological Hobbyist Organization or NACHO, a group that catalogs cryptid accounts in the United States, Canada, and Mexico," Robbins said. "Welcome to CNN, Sebastian."

"Great to be here, Harrison."

"Now you've spent years tracking the Lone Pine Mountain Devil. Could you tell the audience a little bit more about this creature?"

"As you noted in your intro, Harrison, I've been following this cryptid for almost ten years, and despite multiple sightings and accounts, no one has ever captured the creature on video or film. And yet, accounts of the Lone Pine Mountain Devil stretch back through history and are even obliquely mentioned in Native American folklore. Early mid-nineteenth century settlers reported sightings of this reptilian cryptid in southern California's mountain and desert wilderness, often finding the mutilated carcasses of coyotes and bobcats in its wake. Sometimes they'd discover the desecrated heaps of entire convoys of mutilated trappers, miners, or gold prospectors. Franciscan Father Justus Martinez's firsthand account of the slaughter of thirty-six Spanish settlers in 1878 — an incident in which he'd barely escaped with his life — is perhaps the most famous story of this cryptid. When he arrived at Mission San Gabriel Arcángel weeks after the event, he was starving and had nothing but the clothes on his back and a weathered journal detailing the attack. Two months after the massacre, local miners in Lone Pine discovered the corpses of the thirty-six men, women, and children in Martinez's party.

"While there is no consensus on exactly what the Lone Pine Mountain Devil looks like, most accounts describe it as a multi-winged carnivore with razor-sharp talons and venomous fangs.

Yet, most scientists remain skeptical about its existence. They argue that the creature is either just a misidentification of existing species or more likely just a figment of people's overactive imaginations."

"Thank you for your insights, Sebastian," Robbins said.

"Thanks, Harrison," Sanford replied.

The face of a young brunette replaced Sanford's.

Robbins smiled. "Dr. Margaret McGill is a folklorist at the University of Southern California who has done extensive research on the Lone Pine Mountain Devil legend. Welcome to the show, Dr. McGill."

"Thanks for having me, Harrison."

"Dr. McGill, is the Mountain Devil an actual species with hunting grounds in the Lone Pine wilderness, or a mass delusion?"

"I'm sorry to disappoint your audience, Harrison," McGill said, "but the story is a classic Internet hoax. After digging through various historical archives and interviewing people associated with the legend, I tracked the story down to a team of YouTubers who'd made a found-footage video in 2010."

"Thanks, Dr. McGill." Robbins looked directly into the camera. "We'll continue to monitor this story throughout the day."

A scruffy man with white hair and a beard appeared in the screen's right panel. "Up next, Coyote Krieger will provide an update on the World Health Organization's recent allegations that the Chinese had illicitly manipulated CRISPR technology, altering human DNA for the third time since 2018. Coyote, what can you tell us about this developing story thus far?"

Kate turned off the TV. She took several deep breaths. This calmed her until a second later, when she glanced at the time on her iPhone.

She panicked.

"Let's go," Kate said.

She yanked Veronica out of her chair.

"Hey!" Veronica protested. "I didn't finish my breakfast."

"Here's a Pop-Tart," Kate said. "You can eat it in the car."

Frazzled, Kate nearly shoved her daughter out the front door and down the steps into the gaping maw of a media ambush.

A woman with makeup caked on her face like a cheap porcelain doll was the first to thrust a microphone in Kate's face. "Mrs. Weaver, does your father's disappearance make you regret denying him access to his granddaughter?"

Before she'd realized what she'd done, Kate swatted the microphone so hard it sailed into the next yard. The bastards already had their narrative written, and none of it would be true. But that was par for the course. The last time she'd spoken to these jackals, they'd twisted one of her interviews to make it seem like her research "proved" gravitational waves could travel faster than light. The article had nearly sunk her bid for tenure. She'd had to waste valuable research time working with Caltech's communications office to demand retractions. And yet, the morons continued to misquote her to this very day. When journalists faced the divergent paths of working hard to get the truth or writing salacious fantasy, they nearly always chose the easy, sensational route.

Cameras flashed, capturing Kate's assault. She immediately regretted her behavior, for her spectacle had only made the crowd's vise close even tighter as reporters buzzed around her like mosquitos at a blood buffet. All she could do was flare her elbows out and bull through the mob until she could get herself and Veronica into her storm blue Prius.

As Kate sped past scores of palm and Italian cypress trees on her way to work, Pasadena's perfect sunny day did nothing to lighten her mood. Veronica's teachers were not amused when Kate had dropped her off thirty minutes late, but, under the circumstances, they hadn't given Kate any grief. After all, everyone and their mother had known her star-studded father was missing.

Fortunately, Kate's presentation wasn't until 3 P.M., and her first class didn't start till 10 A.M., so she avoided crowds like the plague and quietly slipped into her office by 9:30.

She closed her eyes and sighed. It was the first time today she actually had a chance to think.

Her iPhone buzzed. "Jesus Christ!" she said, exasperated. "Is it too much to ask for one minute of peace?"

Kate grabbed her phone. When she saw the name "Chas" on the display, she rolled her eyes so hard they nearly fell out of her sockets.

"Hi, Chas," she said, "I have a class to teach in half an hour, so make it quick."

"Haven't you seen the news?" he said as if their father's disappearance would make her drop everything and neglect her responsibilities.

"Yes, Chas. I have. The media vans parked outside my home this morning made it pretty fucking obvious. It would've been nice for you to have given me a heads up before I walked into a morning ambush. What do you want?"

"Oh," he said, obviously surprised by Kate's tone. "I just wanted to let you know that Dad has named me as executor for his will."

"I thought Dad was missing. Do you know something I don't?"

"Easy, Kate. I'm just preparing for the worst. That's all."

"Sure you are, Chas. Is that it? That all you needed to tell me?" Kate shook her head in disgust. They hadn't even found a body, and her free-wheeling younger brother was already carving up the old man's estate.

"No need to be all pissy about it."

"Am I in the will, Chas?" Kate fully expected her father had disinherited her, but she still enjoyed making Chas squirm.

"I'm… I'm not prepared to discuss that right now. As you said, Dad isn't technically dead. And I think it's best we try to come together as a family during this difficult time."

"Cut to the point, Chas. What else do you need to tell me?"

"Ah… well, this evening, Mom and I are holding a little soiree at Dad's house. We'd love for you to attend."

Now it all made sense. Chas didn't answer her question about the inheritance because he feared the answer would dissuade her from attending his party. And he'd be right.

"Well, that's all fine and good," Kate said, "but unlike you, I have a child to care for, and tonight just doesn't work for me."

"I figured you'd say that, so Mom and I arranged for a sitter to be at the house."

In one fell swoop, Chas and her mother had completely neutralized the most effective arrow Kate had had in her quiver to skip the event. Kate hesitated. She thought about her father and reflected on their damaged relationship. The shame began to weigh on her. Perhaps it was time to start anew, a time to rally around the family, a time to seek forgiveness and reconciliation. Hell, maybe her father had secretly forgiven her or at least had planned on bequeathing something to his grandchild—a child who'd had nothing to do with their spat. Regardless, Kate concluded it would be healthy to get the family back together.

"Fine," Kate said. "I'll be there."

Ending the call, Kate opened her laptop and went to the benefits section of Caltech's website. If, God forbid, her father did die, she'd have to spend some time away from the office. The university's bereavement leave policy didn't offer all that much time—only up to three days off with pay. And even if special circumstances warranted, such as a need for extended travel, only up to two additional days off were available for a maximum of five days with pay.

Kate couldn't fathom being away from work for that long. Without her, multiple projects would be delayed or completely fall apart. Her mind began to wander. What if they never found her father? Was she content to let things take their natural course, or was she going to do something about it? What if he was still alive? How would she feel if she later learned she could've done something to save him? For all she knew, her father could be lost in the desert, and every day she did nothing, the more likely someone would find his coyote-ravaged remains.

Driven by anguish and guilt, she checked her benefits account to see how many vacation days she'd accrued. The number didn't surprise her: forty days. Kate did not take vacations. She could never bring herself to get away from work. There was too much to do. Too much to miss. Too much risk of not getting tenure. But this time was different.

Kate hadn't yet decided whether to take time off, but she filed away the option. Just in case.

When Kate walked into her Relativistic Astrophysics class—her only class that day—her students seemed distracted, their eyes locked on their smartphones. When she turned from the board to face the class and begin her instruction, she caught a chubby male student snickering. Exposed, his face reddened; he looked away. On another student's smartphone, she glimpsed footage of her knocking the microphone from the reporter's hand.

"Let's get started," she said in a weak attempt to reassert control before adding, "Oh, and put your smartphones away."

Despite the awkwardness of these distractions, Kate acted as the consummate professional, soldiering on through the lecture. Yet, as she mechanically scrawled equations on a whiteboard and droned on about tensor fields and Lorentzian manifolds, she couldn't help but worry about her father.

For lunch at Chandler Café, she tried to eat alone, but Dr. Carley Cabrillo, a Professor of Geology and Geochemistry, crashed Kate's pity party.

"Is everything okay?" Cabrillo said, placing her hand on Kate's back in a faux show of solidarity. An inveterate gossip, Cabrillo poorly camouflaged her self-interested attempt at collecting grist for the rumor mill under the guise of concern.

Kate took a small bite from her veggie burrito, then washed it down with a swig of her kombucha. "Everything's fine."

"You know, I'm not one to pry," Cabrillo said, as she actively pried, "but why aren't you taking time off? These would be tough circumstances for anyone."

Kate took another bite, swallowed, wiped her hands on a napkin, and glared at Cabrillo. "People handle grief in different ways. Some people fall apart. Others whine. People like me take solace in their work. Any more questions?"

Cabrillo's mask contorted into a rictus of outrage. "Well, if you're gonna be like that, then…"

"You can take your meal elsewhere," Kate interrupted, completing Cabrillo's sentence. "Thanks."

"Well, I never..." a flummoxed Cabrillo said as she stood and grabbed her tray.

In case Cabrillo had any doubt about the nature of their relationship, Kate added, "You just did."

Cabrillo huffed as she walked away. After that display, Kate was confident no one else would bother her. Now, she could collect her thoughts in peace and solitude while everyone gawked at her like a rare and dying panda cub at a Midwestern zoo.

When Kate walked into Beckman Auditorium, she expected a room full of well-heeled academic colleagues and civilized local science enthusiasts. Instead, she found a media circus with the monkeys from *Variety* flinging poo from their seats and the august lions of the *Los Angeles Times* serenely stalking the auditorium's periphery in anticipation of a feeding frenzy.

As she shambled toward the podium, half-blinded by an assault of strobing cameras, she spotted Trip Dorn out of the corner of her eye. His face bore a pained expression.

How Kate acted in the next five seconds would determine whether she'd stand or fall. Any hesitation, any sign of weakness would unleash the media's monster. Kate inhaled. She surveyed the audience in the circular auditorium with a sovereign's aura of command. The sudden silence was so deep, she could've heard a gnat sneeze.

The journey from the first word to the last seemed daunting. She forced herself not to think about it. The only way for her to navigate through the morass was to string one stubborn word after the other.

And so she did. Her first two words, "Good afternoon," cut through the tension of the room like a scythe. That got their attention. Those two words snowballed into sentences. Her next sentence expressed gratitude at her invitation. Now she had their interest. Her next paragraph focused on the struggle of a woman succeeding in a male-dominated field. Now, she had their sympathy. She followed that with her love of the beauty and symmetry of mathematics and how it expressed itself in the signs and portents of space and time. Now, she had their love. When she delved into the intricacies of her research on gravitation, she'd earned their adoration.

The truest thing Mack Gavin had ever said of his daughter was that if you dumped her in shit, she'd come out smelling like roses. Today was no exception. When she finished her lecture, the crowd erupted into a standing ovation.

The snarling rush-hour traffic from Pasadena to Malibu did nothing to lighten Kate's mood. Fighting Veronica to get her to finish her homework as she complained every single minute of the drive only added another layer of aggravation to the gridlock.

After several hours, Kate's Prius finally crept up her father's long winding driveway, which curled along a cliff facing the Pacific Ocean. By the time Kate reached the house, it was full dark.

Kate shuddered as a valet approached the car. By her own estimation, she wasn't exactly what one would call a tidy person. The car's floor was carpeted in Coffee Bean cups and candy wrappers. A metastasizing ooze of sugar and dried coffee formed a layer of refuse on nearly every surface. When the handsome young valet, who was obviously a starving actor, motioned for her keys, she said, "No, thanks, I got this," and zipped past him.

The hillside mansion was an affront to both God and man. After Kate passed a gatehouse ringed with a myriad of cryptid statues ranging from Sasquatch to the Chupacabra to the New Jersey Devil, she continued beneath an outbuilding propped up on sandstone pillars. She next entered an open courtyard enclosed by three rectangular sandstone buildings with red-tiled Spanish roofs. Water flowed from the mouth of a Loch Ness Monster fountain at the center of the plaza. Men in tuxedos and women in a mix of fancy alabaster, cobalt, and scarlet gowns ringed the courtyard, clutching champagne glasses under a bank of floodlights. In the compound's far left corner, a clump of cars was cordoned off from the rest of the affair. She parked there and shook Veronica awake. Kate then herded her to the main house's entrance, which faced the outbuilding. She turned and gazed through the pillars. From there, she witnessed the haunting view of a silver full moon shining over the Pacific's dark vastness.

As Kate turned back and entered the main building, she felt the unwelcome gaze of the other guests. She and Veronica had had no time to dress appropriately for such a lavish event. Kate was still dressed in the same professional attire she'd worn at her lecture, a fitted jacket with dress pants. True to form, Chas hadn't bothered mentioning the event would be a black-tie affair.

When Kate and Veronica entered the building, they passed through a parlor with pictures of Mack with all-star quarterback Lincoln McVeigh, actress Lana Lin, and Los Angeles socialite Monika Malone. Mack's housekeeper, Hilda Braun, seemed to materialize from the void to whisk Veronica away to the sitter. For the first time that day, Kate appreciated the help. Hilda was good people.

With nothing left to do, Kate made her way back outside. She snatched a glass of red wine off a tray from one of the many waiters circling the partygoers like gnats. The guests continued to furtively glare at Kate as she tried and failed to blend into the crowd.

Kate hated large gatherings with a vengeance. To take the edge off, she downed three glasses of wine in ten minutes. She wended along the party's periphery, listening to a smorgasbord of inane Hollywood drivel. A rail-thin blonde waif standing ten feet from Kate engaged in a passionate conversation with a wiry middle-aged man with close-cropped gray hair.

"Ugh. What a day," the blonde complained. "My RealReal luxury manager was a few minutes late, so it really threw off my schedule. I've had those handbags for weeks. I need to consign them soon so I can get the latest Saint Laurent satchel bag."

The man registered a bored expression, but the blonde was so self-absorbed, she didn't seem to notice. His eyes caught Kate's. He looked at her and said, "Excuse me, are you Mack's daughter, Kate?"

Kate blushed and nodded. "You got me."

He motioned her over. Kate spotted a slight frown on the blonde's face.

Cornered, Kate had no choice but to join them.

He extended his hand. "Hello, Kate. You look fantastic!"

Kate shook his hand and smiled — awkwardly. "Thank you."

"When was the last time we met?" the man said.

This was the first time they met.

"Was it the Horowitz bar mitzvah?" he continued.

It wasn't. Kate had never attended a bar mitzvah in her life. "I don't think so," she said.

By this point, the blonde's surreptitious grimace had blossomed into a snarling scowl.

The man noticed and said, "Where are my manners? Kate, this is Laurie Tilden. She's the brilliant new star of *Bumper Cars: The Movie*. Remember her. In ten years, she's going to be one of Hollywood's leading ladies."

Kate just nodded. The man gently cupped Kate's elbow. "You know, Kate, we were just talking about our favorite episodes of *The Cryptid Hunter*. I'd be curious to learn which one was yours."

Kate nearly snorted out the wine from her fourth glass. The alcohol's effects had just smacked her like a paddle on a ping pong ball. "Uh… all of them," she lied.

Like the Cheshire cat, the man smiled with his perfect white teeth but not his eyes. "That's what I always say!" He looked at his companion. "Laurie tells me her favorite is the Sasquatch episode. Can you remind me again why it's your favorite, Laurie?"

Now that she was once again the focus of the man's attention, Laurie glowed like a radioactive cesium atom. "The Big Foot episode really spoke to me. The creature is, you know, such a tragic, like, figure. And the way Dr. Gavin humanized him was a really risky creative choice that I think, like, paid off in the end. The episode really pushed the boundaries of what it means to be human. It was, like, so noble. So brave."

Kate ground her teeth to avoid exploding with laughter. When the man immediately changed the subject, she sensed he felt the same way she did.

He ran the back of his hand along Laurie's cheek. "Your skin's so soft and smooth. How do you keep it that way?"

Laurie smiled with the radiance of one of Chernobyl's cooling towers. "Oh, I make my skin a priority, like, every day. I take great care of it. My beautician, Gustaf, has been doing a daily regimen where he rubs eucalyptus leaves and a dash of nutmeg on my cheeks."

"There you are," Chas said as he swept behind Kate. He nodded at the man and his date. "Logan. Laurie. It's a pleasure to see you both. I'm sure you don't mind if I borrow my sister for a moment, do you?"

"Not at all." Logan looked directly into Kate's eyes. "Don't be a stranger. Later this evening, when you have a moment, I have something I need to discuss with you."

"That sounds good," Kate replied with a slight slur. She couldn't possibly imagine what business she had with the man, but it certainly piqued her curiosity.

Chas politely but firmly gripped Kate's upper arm and escorted her back toward the main house.

"Who the hell was that guy?" Kate asked Chas.

"What? You don't know?" Chas said, chuckling. "He's Logan Rhys-Barrington, *The Cryptid Hunter*'s producer. I can't believe you had no idea who he was."

Kate shrugged. "Where's the fire?"

"Huh?"

"You yanked me out of there like it was an emergency. What's so important?"

"Well, I was hoping to talk to you and Mom about something."

"The will?"

"There's no need to be so snippy about it."

"By snippy, you mean direct? And speaking of direct, why the hell didn't you tell me this was a black-tie event?"

"I thought it would be obvious, no?"

"Asshole," Kate said. "No need to drag Mom into this. Let me guess: you want to plan for the worst and start arranging for the distribution of the estate? And you also want to tell me that I'm not in the will, right?"

Chas's mouth twitched like a guppy's — lots of movement, but no sound.

Kate continued, "You shouldn't start planning until the authorities hand us a death certificate and not a moment sooner. And I really don't give a damn if I'm in the will or not. It is what it is. Unlike you, I don't need charity to take care of myself. Plus, I have no interest in his wine cellar or muscle-car collection." Kate turned and rejoined the party.

A few hours later, after Kate had sobered up and Logan had surrendered his floozy to a young actor, Kate approached the producer. "You said you had something to discuss with me?"

Logan flashed his creepy Cheshire cat grin. "I do. Let's go somewhere quiet and find a seat."

Logan's offer sounded ominous, but Kate always carried pepper spray in case things went sideways. By now, the staff had set up several fire pits in the courtyard ringed with chairs. The crowd had dwindled to the point that Logan and Kate were able to find a firepit all to themselves at the far back corner of the courtyard.

When they sat down, Logan grabbed her hands and said, "I'm very anxious about your father's disappearance, and I'm sure you are too. I want to let you know that I'm not going to give up until I find him."

Kate was a bit taken aback by Logan's apparent sincerity. Then she realized that her father was literally the man's goose who laid golden eggs.

"Thank you for your concern," she said. "How can I help?"

Logan waved his hand as if to dismiss her offer. He gazed into the darkness for a moment, then snickered. "Remember what your father used to say when people would ask him what the "W" in his name stood for?"

Kate couldn't help but laugh at the memory. She nodded. "Long as it begins with a 'W,' whatever the fuck I want it to."

He nodded emphatically. "Yes! That's it. Your dad was a real character. I really miss him."

"Do you have any more insight on his disappearance?" Kate asked.

"I do," he said. "The last time he checked in with the studio, he was in Lone Pine, California. He told my team he was heading out to a place called the Alabama Hills to research the Lone Pine Mountain Devil. According to them, he left at twilight."

"Why the Lone Pine Mountain Devil? Why not some other cryptid?"

"You're a very bright woman, Kate. Your father had an uncanny ability to find nuggets of truth in seemingly crackpot theories. This time, he was drawn to the location because of its recent earthquake—a 5.8 temblor on the Richter scale. In the days prior to his trip, he'd been talking to several seismologists about the faults and seismic activity in the region. Mack seemed rather animated about a promising theory that gravitational waves might have been responsible for all the region's quakes stretching at least all the way back to 1872."

Kate winced at the last bit. She was both intrigued and hurt that her father had been examining a fringe theory about a regional gravitational disturbance. She was intrigued because it was her specialty; she was hurt because her father hadn't bothered to reach out to her when he knew she was an expert on the topic.

"What do the police know?"

"Not much. Though they did recover his iPhone and are holding it for evidence."

"What do you know about this cryptid?" Kate asked. "Other than what's out there in the media?"

"I don't quite recall all the details in your dad's notes, but two aspects of Lone Pine Mountain Devil lore really stick out for me. First, Father Justus Martinez's famous account of the creatures explicitly describes them as winged demons. Now, given that Martinez was a priest, one could argue his view is tainted by religious overtones. However, this leads to the second point. Martinez's journal indicates that the creatures didn't attack until the settlers burned trees for light and heat in an area with sparse vegetation. There's an alternative theory that the Lone Pine Mountain Devil is some kind of local guardian, targeting anyone or anything that despoils its habitat—an environmentally-conscious cryptid, if you will. One might argue that having a social conscience isn't a quality exclusive to humanity."

"By the way, do you have any written materials or research my dad pulled together before he disappeared?"

Logan pondered Kate's question for a moment, then nodded. "I do. I can have my assistant scan you a copy and email it first thing in the morning."

"I'd really appreciate that. Thank you."

Kate thanked Logan for his kind words and for bringing her up to speed on the investigation. Then she retired to the main house, where she found Veronica in her guest room tossing and turning on a queen-sized bed. Veronica must've been dreaming about the coyote again. For years, her daughter had had a series of recurring dreams about a coyote looking for his missing star. Kate just shook her head, snuggled up against her daughter, and collapsed into a deep sleep.

By the following evening, Logan's assistant had sent Kate her father's notes. After Kate put Veronica to bed, she pulled out her iPad and scrolled through her father's research. The first few pages contained various eyewitness sketches of the Lone Pine Mountain Devil. They ranged in quality from highly artistic and stylized illustrations of a winged raptor-like dinosaur to awkward stick figure sketches. Several had an exotic look and feel to them: one representation was a mass of wings with no arms or legs; another was a cross between a lizard and an insect.

Karen shook her head at the madness. Her dad had legit-imized these kooks.

After she finished scrolling through the images, she reached a handwritten note in a script she immediately recognized as her father's. At the top of the page, he'd scrawled: "The Lone Pine Mountain Devil: What Is It? Three Candidate Theories."

She read on. Her father wrote:

The consensus view is that the creature has somehow managed to survive the Cretaceous-Paleogene mass extinction sixty-six million years ago – a catastrophe that wiped out over three-quarters of all species on Earth.

In my opinion, this is the consensus view of cryptozoologists for two reasons. First, it is the most scientifically defensible theory. There are fewer variables for respectable scientists to explain and debate. In other words, it's the simplest explanation, the one most likely to balance itself astride the paper-thin blade of Occam's razor. Second, the most common eyewitness accounts of the Lone Pine Mountain Devil often describe a reptilian creature with wings on both its arms and legs. Crypto-paleontologists, in particular, are most likely to gravitate toward this theory because they can easily find evidence of precursor species in the fossil record. In the case of the Lone Pine Mountain Devil, the closest analogue is a microraptor that lived roughly 124 million years ago in China called the Sinornithosaurus. *This species of dinosaur was believed to have had winged arms and legs. It also had grooves in its fangs consistent with other venomous animals. Obviously, this explanation dovetails nicely with native folklore.*

That said, few species survived the mass extinction, particularly those that required terrestrial plant life for sustenance. Those that did endure, such as turtles and crocodilians, tended to occupy aquatic habitats. Not a single one of the hundred and twelve accounts of the Lone Pine Mountain Devil I've examined mentioned or even hinted that the creature was anything other than a land-based animal. Moreover, nothing in the fossil record indicates the Sinornithosaurus *had ever ranged as far west as the North American southwest – even though both China and North America were part of the same continent, Laurasia, during the Cretaceous period.*

While I wouldn't rule it out entirely, I find the Lone Pine Mountain Devil-as-dinosaur theory to be a bit lacking. The evidence just isn't there. I suspect something else is at play here.

Kate laid the iPad on her lap and smiled. Despite her father's ridiculous occupation, she was more like him than she wanted to admit. Like her, he possessed a very skeptical and analytical mind. The thing that had made him so successful and had set him apart from other cryptozoologists was that he applied the scientific method to a field that many serious academics dismissed as pseudoscience. At the same time, he made his scientific inquiries entertaining and digestible for a mass consumer audience.

She scrolled down to the second hypothesis, which her father had labeled: "Demonic Entity Theory."

I hesitate to put these words on paper, for I fear if my fans were to ever read them, the reputation I've spent the past decade cultivating could be imperiled. And yet, I need to exhaust every potential line of inquiry to get to the truth, no matter how crazy or absurd. One such theory is that the Lone Pine Mountain Devil is some sort of supernatural or demonic entity. There are several missing persons reports throughout the region that point to demonic activity. In particular, there's the curious case of the Brown family.

In April 1986, a family of five left Orange County for Palm Springs and vanished somewhere along the way. After family members reported them missing, investigators searched their home and found the lights on, furniture overturned, and bags half-packed. A crucifix had been turned upside down on the wall.

Six days later, the family resurfaced in Lone Pine, starving and dehydrated. When authorities questioned them, all five family members exhibited signs of disorientation and confusion. Under individual interrogation, every one of them provided a consistent story: namely, that they pulled off the highway to get on a back road and got lost. All of them described lights following them in the desert darkness. At one point, the father, Kirk Brown, in a bout of panic, abandoned his Mercury Marquis in a ditch. Then the family wandered on foot until they reached Lone Pine. When the press interviewed Kirk, he said, "Up here in the desert, we had a very peculiar experience." When asked to elaborate, Kirk refused to say more.

Years later, after the rest of the family had died from a mysterious fungal infection, Adam Brown, who had been nine years old at the time of the incident, suggested that demons had emerged from a portal leading to hell and pursued the family. Adam further alleged that these malevolent entities had forced them to participate in a Satanic rite. He was convinced they had cursed him and his family with the sickness that had subsequently killed them. I've reached out to Adam. Unfortunately, I learned he was holed up in St. Joseph's Hospital in a catatonic state.

Putting this incident aside, the strongest evidence underpinning the demonic entity theory comes primarily from Father Justus Martinez's firsthand account of the Lone Pine Massacre of 1878.

Following what most assuredly would have been a deeply traumatic event, Martinez took a vow of silence until he reached the Mission San Gabriel Arcángel, where he relayed his story. I won't repeat the full account here. It's well-documented elsewhere. But what I found most intriguing about the account is Martinez's claim that the victims' souls were "taken from them into the depths of Hell." It's a rather odd yet specific claim. Catholic doctrine at that time and today stipulates that an individual earned salvation through both faith and good works. An attack by some infernal entity would have had no influence on where an individual's soul ended up. Yet Martinez's account explicitly states that these devils transported their victims' souls into Hell. My gut tells me that Martinez didn't mean the metaphorical fire-and-brimstone hell; he meant an actual physical location. I believe these creatures indeed took the settlers somewhere, did something to them, and then discarded their remains in the desert. This, in turn, leads me to the next theory: the Lone Pine Mountain Devils as transdimensional entities.

Kate scratched her head and sighed. She was relieved her father seemed to have quickly ruled out a theory based on religious mumbo jumbo. Still, she couldn't decide if the alternative explanation involving transdimensional entities was even crazier. She still hadn't gotten over the claims that had made him famous in his seminal documentary on Big Sur's Dark Watchers. His theory about the Watchers being shadows cast by hyperdimensional beings seemed crazy to her. Even more so, given all the leaps of logic he made to dispel an alternative theory about how ocean waves and the wind passing through the mountains can generate infrasound that can cause people to hallucinate and experience paranoia.

Rubbing her eyes, Kate realized it was already well past midnight. She had to teach three classes in the morning and had an important meeting with Trip Dorn. She glanced wistfully at her bedroom door. But her curiosity demanded its due. She moved on to the next section of her father's notes.

Other than Father Martinez's account and Paiute folklore, there's not much direct evidence to support this view. However, many of the Spanish settlers, gold miners, soldiers, prisoners at Manzanar, and hikers who'd witnessed the creatures either didn't have the language to adequately describe their experiences, did not understand the concept of transdimensional portals, or some other feature of the Lone Pine Mountain Devil – such as its saurian appearance – had overshadowed all the other salient aspects of their encounters. Whatever the reason, there is a dearth of primary sources that lend credence to this theory.

Kate was surprised at how much she was agreeing with her father. And yet, he still had scrawled a few more meaty sentences about his transdimensional theory. While she didn't expect to learn much more, she read on.

That said, the region's seismic activity has been eerily coincident with Lone Pine Mountain Devil sightings. According to the historical record, almost exactly six years before a pack of Lone Pine Mountain Devils attacked Father Martinez's party, there was a massive earthquake in Lone Pine. At 2:30 A.M. on March 26, 1872, the earthquake struck under a full moon in a clear sky. The town's three hundred residents woke to booming thunder and juddering earth. Their unstable adobe brick dwellings rumbled and tottered until they collapsed in heaps of smoking debris. Fifty-two of Main Street's sixty-two buildings crumbled into ruin. For four hours, over fifty aftershocks leveled any walls that had survived the first tremor. Citizens grabbed whatever belongings they could and fled in terror. By the time it was all over, twenty-seven souls had perished, and the ground had swallowed a local lake. Observers could see a cloud of dust billowing from the town as far as twenty miles away.

It turns out the 1872 quake wasn't the only one to presage Lone Pine Mountain Devil sightings. I've cataloged the region's seismic activity and correlated it with missing persons reports stretching all the way back to 1769. My data includes missives from Father Junípero Serra, letters home from the Forty-Niners in the mid-eighteen hundreds, Father Justus Martinez's 1878 account, newspaper articles about strange incidents at the Manzanar internment camp during World War II, and missing persons reports of lost Pacific Crest Trail hikers.

What I found has been utterly astonishing. In the seven years following a five-plus-magnitude earthquake in Lone Pine, missing persons reports, murders, and accounts of mutilated livestock and wild animals increased by a hundredfold. I've used econometric methods to quantify the correlation between the earthquakes and these events. In my best-fit analysis, I get an adjusted R-squared of ninety-one percent. In other words, an earthquake in the region always presages the arrival of the Lone Pine Mountain Devil. It's a statistical certainty. The only remaining question is: why?

And I believe I know the answer.

Now Kate had to finish reading her father's notes. She may have considered his chosen profession questionable, but he did have a PhD in both evolutionary biology and sociology from Harvard. There wasn't a chance his math was wrong. So what the hell did he think was responsible for these Lone Pine Mountain Devil sightings?

Aside from my daughter, I've reached out to every astrophysicist who studies gravitational waves...

The words wounded her so deeply, she had to stop reading. Kate stifled a whimper. Her eyes watered. Had their relationship gotten so bad that her own father had been too proud to reach out to her? Did he believe she couldn't put her personal grudge aside and behave professionally enough to indulge his curiosity? She needed to continue reading; she had to know how her field of expertise fit into her father's theory.

...I needed to understand if an opening wormhole would generate gravitational waves that could cause this seismic activity. Most of these scientists balked at my question, but Trip Dorn indulged me. When the wormhole was formed, if its far mouth had a higher gravity well than its near mouth, gravitational waves would flow from the high well to the low one. The force of those waves could theoretically cause a seismic disturbance until the wormhole stabilized.

Why hadn't Dr. Dorn mentioned his conversation? Maybe her father had insisted on it. Suddenly, Kate's paranoia about getting tenure reared its ugly head. Maybe Dorn kept things quiet because he didn't want her to know her father thought so little of her abilities? Perhaps Dorn said nothing because he shared her father's opinion.

Kate shook her head. No. She had to stop seeing the worst side of every situation. Her father probably hadn't felt comfortable enough to reach out to her. Either way, it didn't matter now. She possessed the expertise he needed to solve this riddle—a riddle that put his life in jeopardy. So she read on.

But that's the extent to which Dr. Dorn was able to help. For the record, he asked why I hadn't reached out to Kate. He was surprised because her research was even more advanced than his. I was honest with him. I mentioned we had a falling out, and I didn't want to put her in a position where she felt obligated to help me. I still might have reached out to her if Dr. Rosen hadn't called me out of the blue. According to him, the US government had been following my research with interest over the years, and my most recent project was brushing up against something big, something highly classified. Without going into any details, Rosen mentioned that his research indicated the earthquakes were caused by gravitational waves with a localized point source in Lone Pine, California. I expect to meet him in a SCIF at Vandenberg Air Force Base two weeks from now, where he can brief me on some of the more technical details. Until then, I'm heading to Lone Pine to check things out for myself.

A SCIF. Kate vaguely recalled the concept. Dr. Dorn had often complained about several classified government projects that had required him to disappear for hours without a smartphone into an electromagnetically shielded building. That's what it was—a sensitive compartmented information facility.

Now Kate was really concerned. The government, likely the Pentagon or CIA, had been actively monitoring her father. Whatever he was currently working on was so hot, one of their scientists had broken his cover and reached out to him. Not good. Not good at all.

Her father needed her. His life was in danger, and Kate would use every skill she had to find him. She decided then and there to leave for Lone Pine in the morning.

After she had dropped Veronica off at school and had gotten to her office, Kate called Dr. Simon Wong, the head of Caltech's Astrophysics Department, and requested a leave of absence. The slight and soft-spoken Wong offered no resistance. He simply nodded and said, "I completely understand. Take whatever time you need."

Kate's first reaction to his response was guilt. But she brushed it off. Now that she had secured some time off, she had to find someone to care for Veronica while Kate was gone. Her first call was to her mother.

"How you holding up, Mom?"

"Taking it one day at a time," her mother said.

"Listen, Mom, I'm taking a trip to Lone Pine to see if I can help find Dad."

"Why the heck would you ever do that?" her mom responded, surprising Kate with her strong reaction. "Leave it to the pros. They know what they're doing. Plus, I don't want to lose you too."

"I'll be fine, Mom. Listen. I'm calling to ask you for a bit of a favor. I expect to be gone for at least a week. I need someone to watch Veronica. Any chance she can stay with you?"

The line went silent.

"Mom?"

"Honey," her mother finally responded, "I just... can't. It's been hard enough as it is to sleep knowing that I may never see your father again. Having an energetic four-year-old jumping around this house with my fatigue and all my back problems would be a recipe for disaster. It'll also drive Hilda crazy. As you know, Hilda's a housekeeper, not a babysitter. I'll never hear the end of it if I even ask her to consider it. Besides, have you even bothered to ask your deadbeat ex-husband to watch his own daughter? You haven't, have you?"

Kate sighed. "No, Mom. I haven't."

"Well, I think you know what you need to do."

"Okay, Mom. Okay. Love you."

"I love you too, sweetie," her mother replied.

Kate hung up the phone and ran her fingers through her hair. Clenching her jaw, she paced around her office. She knew she was just delaying the inevitable, but she really didn't want to deal with the prick, especially not today and not under these circumstances.

Yet, she didn't have a choice.

After staring at Ray Weaver's name on her iPhone for several minutes, she finally called him.

"Hi, Kate. How're you doing?" Ray answered in his fake enthusiastic affect.

She'd met Ray as an undergrad at Stanford. Now that seemed like a lifetime ago. Since then, their lives had diverged so much they might as well have spoken different languages. She had become immersed in academia while he had followed his sociopathic impulses to be a rainmaking investment banker on Wall Street.

She had no desire to engage with him, so she cut to the point. "As you've probably heard, my father's missing. I'm taking a trip to find him, but I need a place for Veronica to stay while I'm gone. I was hoping you could help me out."

"Normally, I'd be thrilled to spend more time with Veronica," he said, "but I'm working on a really big deal right now. If this merger goes well, I'll really hit it out of the park this year. But it's an all-hands-on-deck situation. I really don't have the time to care for a child."

"But, Ray," Kate countered, "she's your daughter, and you're an investment banker. You could easily afford a live-in nanny. For Christ's sake, you made what? Three million dollars last year?"

"I'm not sure that's any of your business, Kate. Look, I really sympathize with your situation. I really do. But when you sued me for sole custody of Veronica and won, this is the consequence. Can't your mother watch her?"

The smug bastard had a point. And yet, his words still hurt her deeply. He never passed on an opportunity to remind her of that custody battle. Regardless, she knew pushing Ray any further would be a waste of her time.

She made one final plea. "Could you at least pay for childcare while I'm gone?"

He snickered. "To the victor goes the spoils, Kate. A failure to plan on your part does not constitute an emergency on mine."

She vibrated with rage. It took every ounce of self-control for her not to explode. "It's not like I planned for my dad to disappear," she said. "But fine, I'll make do." She ended the call.

Kate briefly considered asking Chas for help, but she knew that was a nonstarter the instant she had the idea. Growing up, from goldfish to golden retriever, every pet Chas had had met a grim fate. The last thing she wanted to do was entrust him with Veronica's well-being.

With no one to care for Veronica, Kate began to have second thoughts about her trip to Lone Pine. Was she being realistic? As her mother had suggested, why shouldn't she let the professionals handle the investigation? What possible difference could she really make? And even if she could make a difference, the only way she could go to Lone Pine now is if she took Veronica. Did she really want to expose her daughter to a potentially dangerous situation?

Kate thought long and hard about her options. She weighed the risks. In the end, she knew she'd blame herself for the rest of her life if she sat on her butt and did nothing.

No. She wouldn't let her father go out like that.

She resolved to leave for Lone Pine that afternoon. Even if it meant dragging Veronica along with her.

After over three hours of driving from Pasadena along US-395, the remote lights of Lone Pine glowed in the valley wedged between the Sierra Nevada's eastern peaks in the west and the Inyo Mountains in the east. Veronica had long since fallen asleep. The sun's red-orange fringe crowned Mount Whitney's jagged peak like a halo. It cast an eerie copper hue on the granite rocks in the valley below.

The Quality Inn came up so fast, Kate nearly missed her turn. After waking Veronica, Kate checked into the hotel and asked the desk clerk, a short elderly man, for a good place to eat. He rec-ommended a steak restaurant called The Grill, located less than a mile down US-395, which doubled as Lone Pine's main street.

At twilight, Kate rolled into The Grill's empty parking lot. It was a weeknight in an isolated desert town, so she wasn't all that surprised. When she and Veronica got out of the car, a winged creature swooped overhead, landing gracefully on an oak tree across the road. It lingered like a harbinger in the growing darkness. Her father would have considered the owl an omen, a warning from an ancestor about some looming danger. For all Kate knew, that ancestor could have been her father, begging her not to mess with the swarming occult forces responsible for his disappearance.

Kate chuckled at how quickly she was succumbing to such superstitious madness. She shook her head as if to snap out of her fugue, grabbed Veronica's hand, and entered The Grill. There, the two had a nice relaxing meal.

Before returning to the hotel, Kate drove further down US-395 until she reached the north edge of town. From there, she turned into the Inyo County Sheriff Substation. The building wasn't much to look at. It had a temporary feel to it, small and nonde-script, like a home in a trailer park. A single squad car occupied the parking lot.

When she and Veronica left the Prius, it was dark. So dark, she could see a clear sky studded with gleaming galaxies full of stars. A crisp breeze made Kate shiver. A tranquil silence smothered all noise. Sometimes Kate yearned for such peace—a life uncomplicated by the hustle and bustle of civilization.

"Mommy, I'm cold. I wanna go home," Veronica said, shattering Kate's brief interlude of peace.

Stroking Veronica's hair, Kate said, "Soon... soon. I just need to talk to the nice men inside first. After that, we'll head back to the hotel and get some sleep."

"No, not the hotel. I wanna go *home*, now!"

Kate hugged her daughter, rubbing Veronica's back vocifer-ously to keep her warm. "I know, honey. I know. We'll get there soon enough. But first, we have to look for Pop-Pop, which means I have to talk to the men inside."

When they walked to the entrance and Kate tried to open the front door, it was locked. To the right of the door, the substation's business hours were posted on a placard. Kate frowned. Apparently, the police were only open for business from 8 A.M. to 5 P.M. Such was the challenge of small towns. While it was annoying, it wasn't a catastrophe. She'd just return in the morning.

The next morning, Kate woke Veronica an hour before sunrise. Kate wanted to familiarize herself with the area, beginning with a quick visit to the Alabama Hills. Veronica wasn't too happy about the early wake-up, but she was too tired to resist. So Kate dragged her daughter into her Prius under the star-spangled darkness. She drove down US-395 until she hung a left on Whitney Portal Road. By then, it was dawn. The towering and jagged gray peak of Mount Whitney loomed high above the valley. Rays of scattered light cast a red-orange glow on the surrounding rocks.

"Mommy, what's that face on the rock?"

Kate pulled over. "What face?" she asked, concerned.

Veronica pointed at a rock cluster several hundred yards behind them, just down the road.

"I don't know, honey," Kate said. "Let's check it out."

Kate got back on the road, did a U-turn, and drove. "Tell me when to stop," she said.

"Stop!" Veronica said less than a minute later.

Kate pulled over to the shoulder and parked. Grabbing Veronica by the hand and crossing the road, Kate came face to face with a massive tan granite boulder amid other large rocks. Spray-painted on the boulder was a giant face: two eyes, two small black nostrils, and big red luscious lips. The left eye had a star circumscribing it. The face reminded her of KISS band member Paul Stanley.

Shaking her head, Kate laughed. "This is why we stopped?"

Veronica nodded and giggled.

"Okay." Kate surveyed the area. The scenery was breath-taking. The rocky desert valley was wreathed by the jagged gray Sierras to the west and the somber brown Inyo Mountains to the east. She took a deep breath, taking in the cool morning desert air.

She gave Veronica a half-hug and said, "I'm going to take a look around, honey. Stay close, okay?"

"Okay, Mommy."

Kate wandered along a sandy trail. She ran her hand against the smooth, rounded rock surfaces forged and tempered through the ages by erosion. She wished she had come here sooner. To get away from it all. It was one of those things she hadn't realized she'd needed until she'd gotten it.

Veronica screamed.

Kate spun toward the sound. She clenched her jaw. Her gut tightened with fear. Kate ran toward Veronica's voice.

When Kate rounded a granite rock as big as two refrigerators stacked on top of each other, she found Veronica standing five feet from three mauled carcasses.

"Step back, honey," Kate said calmly.

When Veronica saw her mother, she rounded the remains and hugged Kate. Kate patted Veronica's back. "It's all right, honey. Everything'll be okay. Just calm down."

After Kate got her daughter to relax, she told Veronica to sit on a nearby bolder and not to move. Taking out her iPhone, Kate took as many pictures of the carcasses from as many different angles as she could. The cops needed to see them because, without evidence, no one would have believed what she saw.

The coyotes' ears had all been ripped off. Their noses were missing. The backs of their necks had been chewed to hell, as if a predator had struck them from above. Oddly, there were no other visible wounds on the animals. The most disturbing discovery was the strange purplish mucous that glazed the corpses. And the smell. It was putrid but different from the reek of rot—more akin to a mix of sulfur and mildew.

Kate was tempted to wipe a sample of the ooze onto a piece of cloth, but she immediately dismissed the idea. She wasn't a biologist and had no training whatsoever in biological contain-ment. Whatever it was, it sure as hell wasn't natural.

Once she was satisfied she had enough visual evidence, she took Veronica to her car and drove to the Inyo County Sheriff Substation, where they waited until it opened at 8 A.M.

When Kate and Veronica entered the substation, a heavyset, bald white police officer with an orange goatee leaned on a counter chatting on his smartphone. Whatever he was discussing, he seemed to be having a grand old time. Such a great time, in fact, that he didn't even look up to see who needed help, which irritated the hell out of Kate.

"Excuse me," Kate interrupted the officer in mid-sentence, "I have an incident to report."

The bald man shifted his attention to Kate. "Pete, I have to go," he said into the phone before ending the call.

His eyes skewered her. It was as if, after having sized her up, he'd found her wanting. He pointed to a clipboard on the counter. "You can start, ma'am, by filling out your information."

It took every ounce of patience for Kate to continue the inter-action without losing her temper. "Yeah, sure. I'll fill it out in a second, but I have some odd evidence to share with you first."

The cop raised his eyebrows as if he was about to say something, but upon seeing Kate's demeanor, he thought better of it. He pulled out a handheld notepad and pen from his back pocket. "Go on."

Kate smiled, pulled out her iPhone, and walked over to the cop.

"My name's Bob Chambless. You?"

"My apologies, officer. I'm Dr. Kate Gavin Weaver. And I'm here to find my father."

Chambless's eyes widened. "Your father? As in Mack Gavin?"

"That's right. I understand you have his iPhone. Could you please return it to me?"

Chambless held out his hands, palms facing outward. "Now, now, Ms. Weaver..."

"*Dr.* Weaver," Kate corrected.

"Dr. Weaver. I'm sorry, but we don't operate that way. We can't release evidence in an ongoing investigation."

"What ongoing investigation?" Kate said. "I thought my father was just missing. What else do you know?"

Chambless clammed up. "Any time someone files a missing person report, it requires an investigation. I'm sorry, Dr. Weaver, but I'm not at liberty to discuss anything related to that case right now."

"Well, why the hell not?" Kate said, raising her voice to a level surprising even her. She took a deep breath and lowered her voice. "My apologies, officer. I drove all the way here from Pasadena to find my father. I'd really appreciate anything you can share with me, no matter how small or insignificant you think it might be."

At that moment, a tall, skinny officer with thinning brown hair entered the reception area from an internal office. "Everything all right here, Bob?" he said to Chambless.

"Ms. —" Chambless began.

Kate frowned.

"I mean… Dr. Kate Gavin Weaver here," Chambless said, putting a particular emphasis on the name 'Gavin,' "is trying to locate her father. She wants his iPhone back."

The skinny officer nodded in understanding. "I'm sorry, Dr. Weaver, but as I'm sure my deputy here has explained to you, we can't release evidence until we complete our investigation."

"And your name is?"

"Oh, where are my manners?" the man said. He held out his hand. "I'm Sheriff Kevin Danaher."

Kate shook it. "If you can't release it, can I at least take a look at it?"

The two men glanced at each other in seeming exasperation.

Before either of them could say another word, Kate placed her iPhone onto the counter. "Let me show you what my daughter and I found thirty minutes ago in the Alabama Hills."

As she showed the cops the images of the mutilated corpses, they registered knowing and worried expressions.

"You've seen this sort of thing before, haven't you?" Kate asked.

The two men remained silent.

"Please. Show me his phone," Kate said.

"I'm sorry, Dr. Weaver, but we can't," Danaher said. "It's against protocol."

Kate heard Veronica sniffling. In half a second, she burst into a sob. Veronica bawled. She crouched like a compressed spring, then broke into a run, wrapping her arms around Danaher's leg. She held on for dear life. "Please," she sobbed. "Help Mommy find my Pop-Pop. Please. I wanna go home!"

Danaher looked down in consternation at the child. He glanced back up at Kate. "Well, seems like your little girl is teaching you a lesson."

"And that lesson is?" Kate said, annoyed at Danaher's paternalistic tone.

"You can get a whole hell of a lot more with tears than jeers."

Danaher's words hit Kate like a box of rocks to the gut with a conflicting mixture of shame and outrage. She stifled the urge to respond because she knew she was partly at fault for Danaher's reaction to her aggressive approach.

He patted Veronica's head. "It's all right, sugar. I'm gonna help your mommy out. But only if you stop crying."

Veronica sniffed and nodded.

Ten minutes later, after Danaher confirmed Kate was who she claimed to be, the two were in Danaher's office. Veronica stayed at the front desk with Deputy Chambless. Danaher had told Kate he didn't want the child to see the video. The implications of Danaher's comment had made her shudder.

Danaher sat in a cheap but comfortable leather swivel chair. He offered Kate a seat in a plastic chair at the opposite end of his desk, then pulled out an envelope and placed the iPhone in front of Kate. Looking her directly in the eyes, he said, "What I'm about to show you is highly disturbing. Steel yourself."

"Wait a minute," Kate said. "How the hell did you gain access to my father's phone when it's password protected? Is that even legal?"

Danaher shot Kate a wounded look. "Ma'am, if we can crack a phone to gain critical information in the course of an investigation, we'll do it."

"I'm sorry, but in a town where the police station only operates during normal business hours, how the hell did you crack Apple's encryption? I mean, it's not like you have a crypto-analysis department in the burgeoning metropolis of Lone Pine."

Danaher scowled at Kate. "Look, lady, I have no obligation to help you at all. If you want to see the video, you're gonna need to check your attitude and ego at the door. Understood?"

Kate shrugged, realizing she'd pushed a bit too far. What was wrong with her? She was normally much better at keeping her emotions in check, and Danaher was only trying to help her. "My apologies. I'm just anxious about my dad."

Danaher nodded. "I understand and sympathize. To answer your question, when we found your father's phone, we called our FBI contacts in Bakersfield and asked for a favor. The agents there used their digital forensics tools to gain access."

"Thank you," said Kate. "I'm really sorry for giving you such a hard time. Let's start over."

Danaher smiled. "No bother. I'd be testy, too, if my father had gone missing and I wasn't getting immediate answers. Anyway, let me show you the video we found. It was recorded about three days ago." He typed in Mack Gavin's password, tapped on the camera app, and hit play.

The screen was black. The video was unusually silent for that time of night. No wind. No chirping insects. No hooting owls. She heard heavy breathing. It sounded like her father was moving through a dense forest at night at a brisk pace. The video panned from left to right across a horizon of faint stars. Out here, she should have been able to recognize the glow of the Milky Way Galaxy or the Andromeda Galaxy's bright spiral. She noticed none of them. In fact, she didn't recognize a single constellation on the screen.

"None of those constellations are visible from Earth. It doesn't make any sense. It's as if he's on some other world... Have you sent any of that footage to an astronomer?"

Danaher shook his head and pointed at the screen. "Keep watching."

Gavin's breathing quickened. Kate heard an odd chattering in the darkness. Something darted from the top of the screen. The video shook, then went dark.

CHAPTER TWO

THE LONE PINE ON THE MOUNTAIN

After viewing the video, Kate couldn't speak. There was a tightness constricting her throat. She couldn't breathe. Her eyes welled up.

"Would you like a tissue?" Danaher asked, holding out a box.

Kate sniffled but shook her head. The last thing she wanted was to come across as some hysterical woman. She was better than that. Harder than that. No one cared if you cried. And it sure as hell wouldn't help in this situation.

She clenched her jaw and told herself to stop being so weak. "I want to help with the case."

Danaher smiled. "I know you have the best intentions, Kate..."

"Dr. Weaver," she interrupted.

"Yeah, yeah. Sorry. Dr. Weaver. As I was saying, I know you have the best intentions, but this is an official police matter. Let us professionals do what we do best."

Kate raised her eyebrow. "If this is your best, then your best is not good enough."

Danaher glared at her. "Dr. Weaver, we are a very small police department in a very small town. We have limited resources and time. And despite these constraints, I assure you we are pursuing every lead. Every angle. We'll let you know if there are any major developments, but we can't promise you anything more than that."

"I see," Kate said. "Could you at least give me a hint where that video was recorded? If not for this case, I'm very curious about the strange constellations I saw. The most logical explanation was that someone recorded that video inside a soundstage. Otherwise, the implications of someone recording that footage under an open sky would be too chilling to contemplate."

"How so?" Danaher said.

"The stars in that video weren't right. Not only would you never see them in Earth's sky, but not in any sky on any world within a hundred thousand light-years. That's why I need to know where you found the video. Please help me put my mind at ease. Please tell me you found it in some local soundstage set up by some Hollywood production company."

"I'm really not at liberty to discuss that right now."

"You don't know, do you?"

Danaher closed his eyes for a moment as if praying for patience.

Kate said, "Look, I can help a great deal with this investigation. I have all my father's notes. You have your evidence. We need to collaborate."

"Dr. Weaver, this is highly unusual. We could always just subpoena those notes."

"Yeah, but that would take time, time you don't have. I promise not to tell anyone I'm working with you."

"I'm sorry, Dr. Weaver, but..."

"If we find my father, I'm sure he'd love to put you on his show. And I would be your biggest champion were we to work together and find him."

Danaher abruptly shut his mouth. He seemed to be considering Kate's not-so-subtle bribe. "Suppose I were to hire you as a consultant. How would you recommend we proceed? I mean, what expertise would I be hiring you for?"

"Well, helping you better understand how my father's mind works for one. I could also connect you with others who knew him well, so you could develop better insights into his behavior. If that's amenable, you could work up whatever your standard contract is, put me through your standard background check, and I would agree to consult for your department for a fixed fee of, let's say... one dollar. That work for you?"

He stared at her for what seemed like a full minute, smiled, then reached across the table and shook her hand. "Deal."

Kate took out her iPad, opened it up to her father's notes, and handed it to Danaher. "Here's what my father's producer sent me. I don't have time to go over it with you now, but I'll email it to you later today."

Danaher quickly scrolled through the notes, nodded, and handed the iPad back to Kate. "Thanks for this," he said.

"Happy to help. Now, your turn. Where was that video recorded?"

"Well, we haven't gotten to it yet, but obviously, it was close to where the hiker picked it up."

"And where was that?"

"On the Pacific Crest Trail."

"Did you speak to the hiker?"

Danaher shook his head. "The hiker was dead."

"How do you know the hiker didn't carry it several miles before you found him?"

Danaher shrugged. "I suppose that's possible. But I think it's safe to assume it was likely very close to where your father disappeared."

"You don't know that. You don't even have any alternative ideas to figure out exactly where the video was recorded, do you?" Kate picked up the phone and clicked on the settings icon. She then clicked on Privacy, then Location Services, scrolled down and selected System Services, scrolled down again, and pressed Significant Locations. Under History, she clicked on Lone Pine, California. Then she clicked on the item corresponding to the date and time of the video. When she saw the resulting location on the map, she wanted to be sick. She showed it to Danaher.

The sheriff stared wide-eyed at the screen. "That's near Mobius Arch."

"Have there been any disappearances around here in recent weeks?"

He nodded. "Worse than that. In addition to your father's case, we've been investigating a series of particularly grisly murders along the Pacific Crest Trail. That particular case is real hush-hush. The FBI's been helping us out there. So far, we've recovered about seven bodies twenty-four miles south of here on Trail Pass."

"How'd they die?"

"Some kind of animal attack."

"Anything like the wounds on the pictures I showed you?"

Pursing his lips, Danaher said, "Yeah, now that you mention it. Their ears were torn off. They also didn't have noses."

"Did a purple substance cover their wounds?"

"Sure did."

"Have your forensics people analyzed it?" Kate said.

"Sure. We just walked it on over to our staff of PhDs at CSI: Lone Pine, and they did the analysis same day."

Kate scowled at Danaher, making sure he understood in no uncertain terms that she was not amused by his poor attempt at sarcasm. "What about the FBI?"

"Look, Dr. Weaver, I've told you over and over again that we're a small department with minimal resources. We collected our evidence and then shipped the bodies to the Inyo County Coroner's Office up in Bishop. If they did any further processing up there, they haven't come back to us yet. If the feds have their way, they may never get back to us. Plus, we just chalked it up to an animal attack and closed the case."

"How did you know it was an animal attack?"

"The wounds had bite marks that weren't human."

"What kind of bites?"

"Do I look like Grizzly Adams?" said Danaher in an outburst of frustration. "I'm not an animal specialist. All I can tell you is they weren't human."

"Do you have a contact at the Coroner's Office in Bishop I can call?"

"Sure," he said. "I'll get it to you once you send me that email with all your father's notes."

Kate grabbed her iPad, located the file, asked Danaher for his email address, then sent him the documents in real-time. "I expect I'll get that contact information sometime today?"

He nodded.

"You also might want to check out those coyote carcasses. I'm sending you a screenshot from Google Maps where we found them. I'd highly recommend you check them out."

"Will do," he said unconvincingly.

"Did these disappearances happen before or after the recent earthquake?" Kate asked.

Danaher scratched his head, thinking. "Now that you mention it, all of them happened after. Probably just a coincidence."

"We'll see," Kate said. "Are there any local experts on Lone Pine Mountain Devil lore I should consult with?"

Danaher slapped his knee and laughed. "You mean like that crazy cryptid stuff your dad worked on?"

Kate's subsequent glare would've made any man regret he'd opened his mouth, let alone what he'd decided to let out of it.

Danaher raised his hands in mock surrender. "Sorry. Didn't mean to make light of your father's disappearance."

"Well," Kate continued, "are there any locals who fit the bill?"

He hesitated. "There's one guy I can think of. Name's Dr. Henry Black. He's a local Paiute man who splits his time between here and Reno. He teaches at the university up there."

"Great. Send me his information along with that of your contact up in Bishop."

"You sure?" Danaher said. "He's a bit of an odd bird. And he's more than likely to just waste your time."

Kate shot him a humorless grin. "Let me be the judge of that."

After leaving the police station, Kate and Veronica returned to the Quality Inn. The cryptic account her father had scrawled into his notes about Dr. Eli Rosen had been nagging her all morning. She had planned to contact Dr. Henry Black later that day, but first needed to learn more about this Rosen character.

To keep Veronica occupied, Kate gave her daughter a Pop-Tart, keyed up the movie "Frozen" into her iPad, and handed the device to her daughter. While her four-year-old eagerly watched the movie, Kate pulled out her laptop.

A quick Google search revealed that Dr. Eli Rosen ran a consulting business called Thoth Intelligence Services catering to military and law enforcement clients. His work focused particularly on cases involving strange phenomena as well as cases that had been impossible for law enforcement to crack with conventional crime-solving methods.

The bio on his firm's website indicated he was a former Associate Professor of Quantum Parapsychology at Princeton at a time when Quantum Parapsychology was part of an interdisciplinary effort between the Princeton Engineering Anomalies Research (PEAR) Laboratory and the Department of Astrophysical Sciences. According to the same bio, his research focused on understanding parapsychological phenomena at the quantum level. More specifically, it attempted to reconcile the principles of quantum mechanics with the theory of gravitation at the quantum scale.

Kate laughed out loud. The man was obviously a quack. But rather than dismiss him outright, she decided to exhaust every possible avenue. So, she looked up some of his research on LexisNexis. To her surprise, he had an impressive array of peer-reviewed articles in prestigious publications such as *Astrophysical Journal*, *Nature Physics*, and *Quanta Magazine*, to name just a few. He had articles with intriguing titles like "Spectral Tensor Analysis of Quantum Shadow Phenomena in Hyper-dimensional Space," "Dark Matter Echoes in Anti-Particle Interactions," and "Gravitational Perturbations at Localized Point Sources." Curiously, these papers stopped appearing in 2007.

She checked the time. It was late morning. She figured she'd review a few of the articles in-depth to assess if he was the real deal. So, she budgeted the rest of the morning and early afternoon to delve into his research. Over the course of three hours, what she found was no less than astonishing.

He had tackled and resolved scientific questions that had baffled his contemporaries for decades. He had a unique ability to leverage disparate scientific disciplines like gravitational theory, quantum mechanics, and superstring theory and meld them together to propose new and intriguing paths for further research in theoretical physics. He also had dared to go well beyond those disciplines to tackle problems in what most of her contemporaries would consider fringe or even pseudo-science, such as astral projection, remote viewing, and telekinesis.

Two things impressed Kate about Rosen: his utter fearlessness in tackling problems most academics would not only avoid but also kill with fire for fear of being ostracized from the scientific community; and the intellectual rigor he brought to novel and multidisciplinary problems. He used highly advanced mathematical methods in his analysis that few people in the world were capable of understanding, let alone able to apply to frontier science.

Kate found his phone number on the website and called him immediately. To her surprise, he answered.

"Hi, is this Dr. Rosen?" she said.

"Hi, Kate," he said knowingly, "I was wondering how long it would take you to call me. And don't call me Dr. Rosen. Eli works just fine."

Kate suppressed her impulse to correct him for not addressing her as "Doctor Weaver". She had much more immediate concerns like: how did he recognize her voice?

"Let's just say I've been following your career with interest," he said. "I must say, I found your recent lecture at Caltech very inspiring."

Kate felt extremely uncomfortable. For all she knew, Rosen was a stalker. "I'm calling about my father."

"I know," he replied. "I'm very sorry to hear about Mack. He's a good man. I've worked with him, unofficially, of course, on several different cases. Many of them are classified. I'm more than willing to share everything about my collaboration with Mack relating to this case, provided it's unclassified."

"Thank you so much," Kate said.

On the surface, everything about Rosen was unappealing to Kate. The photos on his website were anything but flattering. He was bald, heavyset, and had an unmanageable goatee that would break a weedwhacker. He delved in fields where Kate would never dare to tread. And yet, the man still intrigued her. She felt a certain intellectual kinship with him she couldn't explain; an admiration for his bravery in tackling tough but unpopular problems, and awe at the skill he demonstrated in solving them.

"Can you tell me how you've been helping my father these past few weeks?" she asked.

"Of course. A few weeks back, Mack had reached out to me to run by what he thought was an outlandish theory for an upcoming show. He'd had a hypothesis that the region's seismic disturbances were tied to a sudden influx of gravitational waves directed outward from a local point source. And he'd wanted me to investigate this theory."

"Did you?"

"Of course. But I can't really talk about it. My research is classified."

"Eli," Kate said, "my father is missing. Don't you think you have a responsibility to reveal details that could potentially save his life?"

"Kate, that responsibility weighs on me every single day. But our country's security weighs more heavily on my conscience."

"How are the other disappearances, mutilations, and sightings of the Lone Pine Mountain Devil related to these seismic disturbances?"

"I'm sorry, Kate. I literally cannot share anything with you related to Lone Pine. It's all classified. Call me if you learn anything new, and I'll help if I'm able."

"Could you tell me about the nature of your relationship with my father? How long you've known him? When and how you first met him?"

"Kate, your dad is a good man. I've known him for many years, but these questions lead to doors I simply cannot open right now. I'm sorry I can't help you any more than I already have." Rosen hung up.

Now Kate was even more concerned about her father. What on Earth had he gotten himself into? How did his work cross into the national security realm? Whatever it was, it couldn't be good.

True to his word, Sheriff Danaher sent Kate Regina Jimenez's phone number at the Bishop County Coroner's Office and Dr. Henry Black's address. Kate was anxious to meet with Black before the day ended, so by late afternoon, she loaded Veronica into the Prius and drove a little over a mile down Route 395 just past the Best Western to the Lone Pine Reservation.

She rolled by ramshackle homes in various states of disrepair. Car carcasses littered the dirt yards of several dwellings. Once she reached the far eastern edge of the reservation, she parked in a dirt lot in front of a modest trailer. It was neither dirty nor clean. Form followed function.

When Kate knocked on the trailer's front door, a clean-shaven, bespectacled late middle-aged man answered.

Kate extended her hand. "Hi, Dr. Black. I'm Dr. Kate Gavin Weaver. I'd like to ask you a few questions."

Black frowned and crossed his arms, leaning against the door frame. "What the hell is this about?"

Immediately realizing her approach hadn't exactly been the most open or inviting, Kate smiled to lower the temperature. "My apologies. I came all the way from Pasadena to search for my father. I was hoping I could ask you a few questions that might help me find him."

The man stared intently at Kate for several uncomfortable seconds. It felt as if he were testing her — seeing if she would wilt under his withering gaze. But Kate was made of tougher mettle than that. She kept her eyes locked on his for the duration.

Black looked away first, glancing down at Veronica. She grinned. He smiled and laughed. Looking back at Kate, he said, "You must have your hands full with this one."

"Indeed," Kate replied.

"Gavin Weaver, huh?" he said. "Any relation to Mack Gavin, the cryptozoologist?"

"Yes. He's my father. He went missing in this town a few days ago. It's been all over the news."

He shrugged. "I don't really watch TV or spend much time surfing the internet. My work keeps me pretty busy. I simply don't have the bandwidth to follow any of that nonsense."

"So, will you help?"

"I'm not exactly a missing persons expert, but if you think I can be helpful, sure, why not? What exactly do you need?"

"My father disappeared while investigating the Lone Pine Mountain Devil. Sheriff Danaher mentioned you might be able to enlighten me on any old Paiute myths or legends about this cryptid."

"We refer to ourselves as the Numa or Nuumu. We are coyote's children living in the water ditch," he corrected her.

"My apologies. Can you help?"

He nodded. "Come on in."

Kate and Veronica followed Black into the shadowy trailer. Black gestured toward a worn and dusty old leather couch five feet from the entrance. Kate and Veronica sat down. Wrapping her arm over Veronica's shoulder, Kate watched Black like a hawk and regretted putting herself in such a sketchy situation. He walked toward a kitchenette on his left and opened the refrigerator, which creaked like a dying old man, parched and starving in a trackless desert. "Would you like anything to drink? I have iced tea, orange juice, and Diet Coke."

"I want orange juice," Veronica said.

Black shot Veronica a wide grin. "Anything you want, Princess." He pulled out a glass from a cupboard and filled it with orange juice, then walked over and handed it to her. He glanced at Kate. "And you?"

"No, thank you," Kate said. "About the Lone Pine Mountain Devil: what kind of lore do the Numa have about the creature?"

Black shook his head, turned around, and walked back toward the kitchenette. "Woman, you are all work, no play, all the time. Take a deep breath and relax a little."

Kate bristled. "Excuse me for having a sense of urgency when my father disappeared in a desert."

He held out his hands in mock surrender. "Look. I just drove down from Reno about thirty minutes before you arrived. I'm a little tired and cranky. Give me a break, will ya?"

"I'm sorry. What is it you do in Reno?"

"I'm a Professor of Linguistics. My specialty is the Western Numic branch of the Uto-Aztecan language family. I also teach the occasional anthropology course on the ethnography of the Numa people. I visit Lone Pine often but spend most of my days in Reno. I like to come here to keep my language skills sharp by spending time with the tribe's elders."

Kate nodded.

Black popped open a can of Diet Coke and took a big gulp. He stared into space for a moment as if in concentration. Then he spoke. "There's not a lot in the record about the Mountain Devil, but you can find hints of it if you look hard enough. My ancestors have often spoken of guardian spirits who presided over the Alabama Hills, tearing apart any predators encroaching upon their sacred hunting ground — human or otherwise. I really don't know much about the exact nature of these beings, but I believe they're real. I believe there's something out there. But what exactly it is, I have no earthly idea."

Kate began to believe Sheriff Danaher's warning. This was turning out to be a colossal waste of time. "I see."

Black scratched his head. Again, he seemed to be pondering something. "Look. You aren't the first person to ask me this question. And you certainly won't be the last. Nothing immediate comes to mind, but my people have passed down many apocryphal tales that could be obliquely related to the strange disturbances associated with the creature. For instance, there's a story of a Numa trapper that's been passed down through the generations. Each day, the trapper would return to find his traps empty but the bait gone. After days of no success, his trap snared a large coyote. When the trapper was about to slaughter the animal, it spoke to him in Numa. It said, 'My friend, my people have found it necessary to warn you. Do not trap us. Don't carve the skin from our bodies and sell them for your happiness.... You may not know I miss a star. I have combed the cosmos without success. I will show you its place in the heavens. There will be a division in the universe which I will cause to be known later.'"

"What does that story even mean?"

He shook his head. "It's not clear. I believe that the coyote wasn't just a coyote. Maybe it was a creature that looked like a coyote but wasn't. Maybe the coyote had been possessed by some guardian spirit. Either way, the coyote was lost. It was a long way from home. But it also offered a warning. What that warning was, I can't say."

Kate resisted the urge to grimace and shifted in her seat, not seeing how his tale could possibly relate to her father's disappearance. "Are you familiar with the story of Father Justus Martinez?"

"I don't know. Can you remind me?"

She relayed the full story, ending with, "I figure the exact date of the occurrence was on March 13, 1878 — Saint Roderick's Feast Day. If the copper miners discovered the thirty-six rotten corpses two months later, that would imply they found the bodies on or about May 12, 1878, by my reckoning."

"Ah, yes. I do vaguely recall that tale. The miners had probably come from the Alabama-Mohawk Mine, which is roughly five miles northwest of Lone Pine on the northern edge of the Alabama Hills. At the time, the mine primarily contained gold but also held copper deposits. The mine's workings included underground openings comprised of a three-hundred-foot passageway leading into a mine that connected with a shaft over a hundred feet from the mouth of the mine..." Black looked up. "Oh, sorry. Sometimes I can get lost in the minutiae of local history. Regardless, many strange things do indeed happen under a coyote moon."

"Coyote moon?"

"It's a term my people use to describe the young moon in February or March," Black replied. He looked back over at Veronica. His eyes widened. He took another swig of his Diet Coke, then walked over to the little girl. He crouched down and patted her head. Then he stood up and turned back toward Kate. "You know, the power of the shaman reveals itself early in life. In recurring dreams, it wanders through the child's mind, just beyond her grasp. It has substance but also is ephemeral. It will haunt your child until she understands its meaning. With the onset of adolescence, the young shaman begins to comprehend the songs, which first manifest themselves as a vague and distant humming. Later, they take on form and substance. Over time, the unconsciousness drifts to the subconscious, until by adulthood, it becomes ingrained in the conscious mind. I sense this power in your child. Protect her well, for others will sense it too."

Black's last words made Kate shiver. She'd found the entire encounter strange and unsettling. She silently admonished herself for not paying more attention to Sheriff Danaher's warning. For all she knew, the man could've been some kind of cultist.

Kate pulled out her iPhone and made a big show of checking the time. "Oh my," she said, "it's getting late, and I have another appointment." She yanked Veronica's glass of orange juice out of her hands. Her daughter squealed in protest.

"I see," Black said, in a way that made it clear he was unconvinced.

Kate shook his hand. "Thank you very much for your time."

He nodded, the hint of a scowl betraying his otherwise emotionless face.

As Kate was nearly out the door, he said, "Remember. Protect that child. If the wrong being senses her gift, you could all be in danger."

"You bet," Kate muttered as she slammed the door shut and sped into a slow trot to get back to her Prius.

The first thing Kate did when she and Veronica returned to the Quality Inn was to call Regina Jimenez at the Bishop County Coroner's Office. After introducing herself, exchanging the usual pleasantries, and explaining why she was calling, Kate got straight to business. "My apologies in advance, but I have a rather odd question."

"Go on," Regina said.

"When you analyzed the purple residue on the bodies you recovered from the Pacific Crest Trail, what sort of results did the lab return?"

"How'd you know about that?"

"I found the secretion on three dead coyotes this morning in the Alabama Hills. When I reported it to the Lone Pine Police, they indicated they found the same substance on those corpses. They told me to call you if I had any further questions."

"I see," Regina said. There was a long pause.

"Well," Kate pushed, "what did the lab analysis reveal? What exactly is this substance?"

"I'm really not sure I should be discussing this."

"Why not? I won't tell anyone. Please. My father's missing. It could really help."

There was another long pause. Regina took an audibly deep breath. "Okay. But you didn't hear it from me."

"I promise not to say a word."

"The substance contained spores. Spores we've never encountered before."

"Spores your lab has never seen before?" Kate asked to clarify.

"Spores *no* lab has ever seen before. No lab on Earth."

"Jesus. Could you elaborate?"

"All the lab could tell me was that they were similar to spores dispersed by fungi—but different. The lab technician described it as belonging to some sort of fungal-animal hybrid. After that, she refused to elaborate any further. She told me a government official had visited the lab and seized the results. He'd instructed her never to speak of them to anyone. I'm amazed she'd revealed as much as she had. A day later, three feds showed up here and removed the bodies from our morgue. They also warned me never to speak a word of this to anyone."

"What specific agency?" Kate pressed.

"I have no idea. The only reason I released the bodies was I got a call directly from the Governor's office ordering me to do so."

What the hell have I gotten myself into? Kate thought.

"I see," Kate said. "Thank you for your time."

She hung up the phone none the wiser. Just when she'd thought she'd started to get a handle on the case, some new fact pattern emerged that completely scrambled whatever working theory she'd assembled. Now it was back to the drawing board — again.

The next morning, Kate and Veronica went to the place in the Alabama Hills where her father had recorded his last video. Kate traveled along Whitney Portal Road past lines of cottonwoods. She drove by the rock face where she and Veronica had discovered the coyote carcasses. Soon, she turned onto a dirt road and headed toward a string of granite formations. Before her, strata of rock stacked atop one another like layers of multi-hued reddish soft-serve ice cream. Several RVs clustered at the base of these magnificent rocks — campers enjoying the natural beauty, oblivious to the hidden danger lurking in the desert wilderness.

Kate followed Google Maps until she reached the Mobius Arch Loop Trailhead. She and Veronica grabbed some water bottles, left the car, and got on the trail. The trail wound through a gully and then around a series of rock formations. Kate followed both the trail and her GPS to ensure she wouldn't get lost. It took less than twenty minutes to reach the arch.

This early, Kate and Veronica had the area all to themselves. The sun had been up for no more than an hour, its rays reflecting off the rust-colored rocks ahead. To the west, Mount Whitney's snowcapped gray granite peak towered over the valley.

Kate circled the arch to get a feel for the area. Because of the darkness, it was difficult to tell exactly where her father had recorded his video. She found no signs of struggle, no blood, no torn clothing. The incident might as well have happened a million years ago.

Curious, Kate climbed up to the arch. It was literally shaped like a Möbius strip — a form rendered by taking a single strip of material, half-twisting one end, then joining it to the other end to form a loop.

Wind swirled through the rockpiles of the tranquil valley. Kate stood on the arch's eastern face. Through the arch, she faced west, where she could see Mount Whitney in all its splendor. It was like peering through a looking glass and seeing a new world on the other side.

She then took Veronica to the opposite side of the Arch and looked east through the stone portal, where she could see the auburn Inyo Mountains.

"Mommy, I want to see the big gray mountains through the arch again," Veronica said.

Kate smiled. "I suppose it wouldn't do any harm. Be very careful when you go over to the other side."

"I will, Mommy."

Veronica carefully climbed around to the arch's eastern face.

Kate continued to stare out toward the Inyo Mountains, waiting to see her daughter. After about a minute, Kate started getting nervous. "You okay over there, honey bun?"

"Yeah, Mommy. I'm fine."

Kate breathed a sigh of relief. Yet, she still couldn't see Veronica's face through the arch. "I thought you were going to look through the arch, honey?"

"I am, Mommy. I don't see you. You need to look through the arch too."

Kate climbed closer to the arch. She stuck her head through it, scanning left, right, and down. Her gut roiled. "Honey, can you hear me?"

"Yeah, Mommy. I still can't see you."

This is impossible, Kate thought. She should've been able to see her daughter.

Trying a different approach, Kate asked, "What do you see right now?"

"Not much, Mommy, just lots of trees. It's hard to see because it's nighttime in there."

Kate hesitated, unable to fully process or make sense of the implications of Veronica's words. Trees? Impossible; they were in a damn desert. There was a long uncomfortable pause.

Veronica screamed, "Mommy, Mommy! I see eyes. They're coming for me."

Kate's pulse quickened. She bit her tongue. The salty taste of blood saturated her senses. Kate whipped around the arch. There, she found her daughter staring into the portal. She whisked Veronica away from it, wrapping her daughter in her motherly embrace. Kate hugged Veronica with all her might, relieved her daughter was still with her. Veronica sobbed.

"It's okay, honey. You're safe now," Kate said in an effort to reassure her child.

Once Veronica had calmed down and caught her breath, Kate said, "Now tell me what you really saw."

"I saw eyes, Mommy. Big bright glowing yellow eyes. They watched me from the dark. From the other side."

Kate turned toward the arch and peered through it. She saw what she had expected to see: a beautiful view of Mount Whitney's chiseled gray rock faces.

Crouching to be eye-level with Veronica, Kate grabbed her by the shoulders and bored into her daughter's tearing eyes. "There's nothing there. There are no eyes. No darkness. It's all okay."

Tentatively, Veronica crept up the rock for a better vantage point. She peeked through the arch as if expecting something to reach out and grab her. "I...I don't understand, Mommy. Now all I see is the gray mountain. Where did the nighttime place go?"

Hugging Veronica again, Kate said, "I don't know, honey. I don't know. But whatever you saw, it has something to do with why your Pop-Pop is missing."

Gazing through the portal, Kate could think of many possibilities, but not a single one of them made any sense.

The morning's events had rattled Kate. So much so that they had fled the Alabama Hills and holed up in their hotel room. Kate decided to take the day off to rest and relax. Yet her mind kept spinning. Generating impossibilities. Attempting to reconcile the irreconcilable.

After wasting a day without coming to a resolution, Kate's phone rang at 7 P.M. Sheriff Danaher's name appeared on her iPhone display.

"Hello, Sheriff," Kate answered. "How can I help you?"

"Well, Dr. Weaver, I really don't know how to explain this, but your father wandered out of the desert and into The Grill."

Kate was at a loss for words. A feeling of euphoria surged through her body.

"Dr. Weaver?" Danaher said.

"Ah… yes. Sorry. Did you say my father wandered back into town?"

"I did," Danaher said, chuckling.

"Is… is he all right?"

"He's a bit disoriented but seems to be healthy. We're with him at the restaurant but need to get him down to the station before the press gets wind of it and mobs the place."

"I understand," Kate said. "I'll leave immediately and meet you at the station."

Dr. Mack Gavin, the world-famous Cryptid Hunter, stood facing the police station's front counter. He reeked of stale sweat and filth, his clothing soiled and torn.

For the first time in her entire life, Kate felt sorry for her father. She couldn't imagine what he must've gone through over the past several days. The fact that he'd managed to survive this long was no less than a miracle.

"Dad?" Kate said tentatively. She still couldn't believe he was here. When he faced her, the feeling only intensified.

An expression of recognition alighted his face. She could feel it. "Kate?" he said. "Is that really you?"

"Yes, Dad. It's me."

She launched herself two steps forward and hugged her father with the same force she'd embraced Veronica with that morning. She squeezed him as if she'd never let him go again.

When Kate finally released him, her father spotted Veronica and said, "Is that my granddaughter?"

A tear streamed down Kate's cheek. She was so overwhelmed with emotion, she couldn't speak. She nodded instead.

A filthy Mack Gavin limped over to Veronica, crouched, and gave her the sweetest hug Kate had ever seen.

Kate looked over at Danaher and Chambless. "Has he eaten yet?"

Danaher nodded. "Yeah. We bought him a nice steak at The Grill."

"Thank you for that," Kate said. She reached into her purse. "How much do I owe you?"

Holding up his hand, Danaher said, "Don't worry about it. Our pleasure."

"Do you still need him here?" Kate said. "My hotel room has two beds. He can sleep in my room tonight if that's all right with you."

Danaher exchanged a glance with Chambless, then looked back at Kate. "As long as he's here for questioning first thing in the morning, I don't see an issue with that."

"Thank you so much," Kate said.

"However," Danaher continued, "I'd recommend putting a police car outside your hotel just in case. Deputy Chambless here would be happy to do it."

Chambless added, "Really, it's no trouble at all. Just part of the job."

"I really appreciate the offer," Kate said, "but I don't think that'll be necessary. I promise I'll bring him here first thing in the morning."

"Here's some of my clothing he can wear while he's still in town." Danaher handed her a large brown paper bag.

"Thank you so much," Kate replied.

Shortly thereafter, Kate, Veronica, and Mack left the station. Kate felt compelled to question her father as they drove back to the hotel, but she restrained herself. Best to give him time to clean up and feel human again before bothering him.

Once her father had showered and put on Danaher's clothes, Kate lost her patience. "Dad, can we talk about what happened?"

He laid down on his bed and stared at the ceiling without acknowledging Kate's question.

She tried again. "Dad, please. We've all been worried sick about you. I have so many questions. I just need to know. I know things have been tense between the two of us, but your disappearance has really made me reconsider our differences. And frankly, it's not worth it for us to hold such a longstanding grudge. I love you, and I miss you. And your granddaughter needs to know her grandfather. Don't you agree?"

Her father continued to stare at the ceiling. It was as if he wasn't there; he seemed like nothing but a shell. Kate tried to rationalize his behavior. He'd been through a terrifying ordeal. For all she knew, it could've been so horrifying, he simply couldn't bring himself to relive it. And without knowing what he'd endured, who was she to judge? Instead of continually pestering him, she decided to leave him alone. Maybe a good night's sleep would give him the distance he needed to open up. Plus, she had to remind herself that the worst was over. Her father had returned. So she went to sleep with renewed hope that they'd sort it out in the morning.

When Kate woke, Veronica and her father were gone.

Electrified with panic, Kate checked the bathroom. Nothing. She opened the closets. Finding no one, she threw on jeans and a tee-shirt, grabbed her phone and keys, and rushed to the hotel lobby.

"Everything all right, ma'am?" the manager said.

"No. Everything's not all right," Kate replied. "I'm looking for my father and four-year-old daughter. Have you seen them?"

"Funny you mention that. An old man left carrying a sleepy little girl at about 3 A.M. She looked to be about four years old."

"Where'd they go?" Kate demanded.

"I'm not sure. The old man didn't say anything. Just walked out the front door."

Kate scowled at the man even though she knew deep down he didn't deserve it. He was just doing his job. She pulled out her phone and called Danaher to alert him to the situation. Danaher acknowledged the report and told her that no one was currently at the station, so the quickest way to reach him was for her to meet him and Chambless at the Mobius Arch Trailhead. Then she ran out of the hotel and smacked right into a media ambush.

Kate sharpened her elbows and shoved her way through the cameramen and reporters until she reached the safety of her car. As she backed out of her parking space, she narrowly missed hitting three reporters. She was relieved but not sorry. She maneuvered her Prius around the swarming journalists and headed for the Alabama Hills.

Her decision to invite her father into her hotel room haunted her. How could she have been so stupid? Yes, he was her father. The man who'd raised her to be the successful woman she was today. But the more she thought about it, the more she realized she'd missed the signs. What she had interpreted as her dad's refusal to speak must've been something else, some sort of catatonic state or trance. She should've been more observant, more careful. Now, Veronica was missing, and Kate felt lost and helpless. Her innocent little girl was now at the mercy of forces beyond her understanding. With all the strange happenings in Lone Pine, she couldn't figure out what was up and what was down. Everything was topsy-turvy.

She wanted to believe that she was just overreacting. Her father had probably just taken his granddaughter out for an early hike to make up for lost time. Maybe he took her for an early run. The more she fabricated these scenarios, the more she realized how implausible they were. Her father had been lost in the desert for five days without water or food, then had returned without any explanation. Compounding that mystery were more strange and unexplained phenomena: the purple secretion linked to attacks from an unidentified predator, the spike in disappearances associated with local earthquakes, the yellow eyes gazing at Veronica through the portal.

No. Kate wasn't overreacting. She was afraid. Very afraid. Something was deeply wrong with her father. He wasn't the same man who'd raised her. Kate fought against a surge of panic. Her protective maternal instincts took over. She would find Veronica no matter what, no matter how long it took, no matter what the cost.

An ambulance zipped by her on Whitney Portal Road, its lights flashing with a fierce urgency that only intensified Kate's worry. She put her foot on the gas and sped up, anxious to get help.

When Kate rolled into the Alabama Hills campsite, she entered pandemonium. A slew of ambulances was parked next to RVs. Paramedics were loading bodies on gurneys. The lights from a police car flashed at the Mobius Arch Trailhead. Danaher and Chambless were speaking to a disheveled and disoriented woman.

Kate had stumbled upon a slaughter.

After she'd parked her Prius, it took every ounce of her will not to break into a wild sprint toward Danaher and Chambless.

"What the hell happened out here?" Kate said to them, "and why didn't you say something about this on the phone?"

"There was some kind of animal attack," Chambless said.

"We didn't tell you about it, Dr. Weaver," Danaher added, "because we didn't want to alarm you."

Surveying the carnage, Kate spotted three bodies — one of them a child. A horrible thought invaded Kate's mind. "You... you didn't find Veronica's... body, did you?"

"Jesus," Danaher replied. "No, we didn't. Let's not jump to conclusions. We'll find your daughter. I promise."

"Did... did they have the same wounds? Were these victims covered in a purple discharge?"

"Yes, and yes," Chambless said.

"Let me see them," she said.

Danaher touched her shoulder. "Dr. Weaver. Please, don't do this to yourself. It will only worry you more."

"Take me to the bodies!" she screamed, instantly regretting her loss of emotional control.

"Okay. Okay," Danaher said. "Follow me."

While Kate would never openly admit it, Danaher was right. This abattoir only compounded her anxiety about Veronica. The only thought now keeping her sane was the fact that her father had somehow survived whatever had been killing people and animals in the region. She convinced herself with every ounce of her will that both her father and daughter were still alive somewhere in the Alabama Hills.

Kate steeled herself for what she was about to witness. She needed to see it; she needed to understand what she was up against.

Three black body bags lay in the dirt. Chambless squatted and unzipped one, revealing an old man. Kate gasped. "Is this all of them?"

Chambless shook his head. "It's still early. So far, we've found these and seven more, but we're not done yet."

She nodded, then examined the old man before her. Something had shorn his nose and ears clean off his wrinkled head. Kate shivered. Then, realizing it wasn't her father, she relaxed. Overwhelmed by the sight, Kate looked away. Then she forced herself to look again. A translucent purple jelly glazed the man's face. If she focused intently enough, she could see tiny speckles like pepper spice embedded in the ooze.

Spores.

She turned to Danaher. "Do you have cotton swabs and an evidence jar?"

He nodded, then yelled out to a man wearing blue latex gloves and goggles. "Rodriguez, get over here. I need you to take a sample."

The man trotted over to the scene, bent down, and examined the body. He looked back up at Danaher. "What kind of sample did you want me to take?"

"Put that purple stuff in a box," Danaher replied.

"Don't we have explicit instructions from the feds not to collect any more samples? In fact, they were pretty clear we should avoid interacting with the substance in any capacity going forward."

"Yeah, yeah, yeah," Danaher said. "This lady works at Caltech. She's with the government. It's fine."

Kate didn't know whether to be furious with Danaher for not telling her about the feds' guidance or thankful he lied so she could get a sample of the mucous for independent analysis. She decided to be pragmatic and roll with Danaher's deception. But she'd make damn sure he told her everything afterward.

Rodriguez scraped a sample, placed the swab into a small cardboard box, and handed it to Kate.

"Thank you," she said, securing it in her purse.

After Rodriguez left, Kate turned to Danaher. "Sheriff, I know you've got your hands full here, but what about Veronica and my father?"

"My gut tells me it's all somehow related to this, and when we find answers here, we'll find answers there," he said. "Regardless, I put out a BOLO immediately after you called. I also registered Veronica in the AMBER alert system. So, if she isn't in the area—though I strongly suspect she is—we'll find her. Trust the system."

Kate nodded and rubbed her eyes. She wanted to argue with the man. She wanted to rage and scream at him for not putting the life of her sweet little girl ahead of everyone else's. But she knew it wouldn't do any good.

"Is there anything I can do to help you find Veronica?"

Danaher grabbed Kate's upper arm in a gesture of reassurance. "Yeah. Actually, there is. Don't blame yourself. Stick around here with us. We'll share what we find. Then we can all use the information to find Veronica and Mack. It also won't weigh on you as much if you keep yourself busy."

Despite their initial meeting, Danaher was really starting to grow on Kate. So much so that she regretted how dismissive of him she'd been in their first interaction. "Thank you for the advice, Sheriff. I really appreciate it."

Kate spent the rest of the day shadowing Danaher and Chambless as they took a grim accounting of the carnage. She didn't envy them. For the next week, they'd have a caravan of next of kin coming to town to identify the bodies.

By late afternoon, after watching the examination of the fifteenth corpse, Kate had an epiphany. She couldn't shake Veronica's account of the nighttime place; the place with trees that her daughter had claimed to see when looking through Mobius Arch. For a moment, Kate suspended her disbelief. Why would her daughter have seen a forest in the desert? As her mind raced through the possibilities, only one thing could explain the anomaly—a wormhole. What if the earthquakes in the region had been caused by gravitational waves emitted from the opening of a wormhole? What if the point source of that wormhole was at Mobius Arch? What if the arch *was* a portal to another dimension? What if something had emerged from it and taken both her father and daughter?

To Kate, these leaps of logic seemed insane. Yet, it was the only string of logical propositions she could construct to explain all the available evidence. Gravitational waves had been detected in the region during the earthquakes. Seismic activity had preceded every account of the Lone Pine Mountain Devil throughout all recorded history. And people only began to disappear after the quakes.

Under the pink and orange glow of the setting sun, Kate made her decision. If she was right, she'd find her father and Veronica at Mobius Arch. She ran along the trail as if their lives depended on it.

The sun had fallen beneath Mount Whitney's serrated peak. The crimson glow of twilight suffused the sky. The air chilled, and the wind whipped and whistled through the valley.

Several minutes into her run, Kate could barely breathe. She stopped for a moment, bending forward and grabbing her knees to catch her breath. She only had less than a quarter-mile to go. She felt guilty for stopping so soon, but she knew she'd do her father and Veronica no favors if she rushed headlong into danger. As she approached her final destination, she had to be more cautious for who knew what awaited her there.

A shadow traced along the rocks ahead. But was it a shadow? It had moved so fast, Kate couldn't decide what she'd actually seen. Whatever it was, it didn't matter. She had to get to Mobius Arch. And nothing on heaven or earth would stop her.

Night came on quickly in the desert. Were it not for the faint starlight, Kate wouldn't have been able to see as far as her hands. When she looked to the heavens, she could vaguely make out the Andromeda and Triangulum galaxies. At least she could be sure she was still on Earth... for now.

The encroaching darkness had swept in so quickly, Kate began to have doubts. Here she was, all alone in the dark. Nearly a score of human beings had been summarily slaughtered just hours earlier. Something murderous lurked in the sinister darkness. And if it crossed her path, she had no idea what she'd do.

As she shambled through the gloom, she regretted coming out here all alone at night. How could she have been so stupid? So shortsighted. So reckless.

She approached the final turn on the trail to Mobius Arch. A pale glow leaked through the darkness. Kate's pulse quickened. Her heart fluttered with both fear and anticipation. When she rounded the corner, the Mobius Arch cast a shimmering white light. Silhouetted against that light were two figures: a man and a child.

Kate's heart stopped. She froze like a deer standing in front of a tractor-trailer.

Her father's voice barked and grunted in some arcane and ancient guttural language. Veronica held his hand tightly. She stood cowering before whatever monstrosity lurked on the far side of the portal.

This sublime vision mesmerized Kate. The sight she was witnessing inspired a sense of awe and wonder. *So, this is a wormhole,* she thought.

As her eyes adjusted to the light, for the merest of moments, she glimpsed movement on the other side of the portal. A flash of a membranous wing. A blur of jaundiced eyes. So many eyes. Gazing from some twilit realm on the edge of forever.

A miasma of malevolence washed over her. It was tangible. Real. Something from beyond the portal had reached into her mind and made her feel this. Made her grovel in its supreme corruption and filth. It had manifested its intentions to her, and it had possessed such power that it cared not that she knew. It would do what it willed.

Gunshots!

Kate snapped out of her trance. Her father and Veronica began to march toward the rippling portal.

Veronica glanced over her shoulder. Tears streamed down her face. "Mommy!" she yelled.

Against all caution and reason, and with complete disregard for her life and safety, Kate rushed forward. She wrested Veronica from her father. She spun on her heel, holding onto Veronica's hand with all her strength. But like Lot's wife at Sodom, Kate looked back. She came face to face with her father. His face glistened with sticky purple slime. But that wasn't the worst part. The worst part was the menace exuding from his pure purple eyes, a menace that came from beyond her father's consciousness. Something malignant had infested him. Kate couldn't explain how she knew. She just did.

In that instant, Kate knew her father was lost. Any attempt to save him guaranteed death.

She threw Veronica over her shoulder, spun around, and fled for her life.

CHAPTER THREE

A PORTAL TO HELL

It took every ounce of Kate's focus to stay on the path. She had an urgency to run faster but knew if she did, she'd risk getting lost in the desert without supplies or water. She had to optimize between the probability of a slow death and a quick one.

Veronica sobbed. Every bump and turn elicited a punctuated gasp from the child. The drive to survive hijacked every other mental faculty Kate still possessed. It overrode everything. Within that survival directive, paramount was a mother's need to protect her child.

Kate stopped looking down at the path. She was moving too slow. Instead, she oriented on the strobing ambulance lights in the distance. She ran faster, picking up her pace. She fumbled in the darkness, tripping and stumbling over stones she couldn't see. And still, she ran, hunched with her daughter balanced precariously over her shoulder.

A horrifying shriek pierced the darkness. A second shriek answered in sympathy. The faint sound of heavy footfalls echoed in the night. Kate continued to run. Her legs grew heavier. Her shoulder, sore from supporting Veronica, flared in pain. Kate had to stop to catch her breath. For relief, Kate slumped Veronica over to her opposite shoulder.

More shrieks resonated in the sinister dark. They grew louder and more frequent. More urgent. Once she'd secured Veronica in place, Kate began to run again toward the lights.

Ahead, two flashes temporarily blinded Kate.

Gunshots!

A series of horrifying conclusions inundated Kate's frantic mind. If Danaher and Chambless were firing their weapons, the creatures had returned to the campgrounds. And if other creatures were chasing her from behind, she was surrounded.

In such a scenario, Kate reasoned, she only had one option for survival: run to the sound of the guns. And so she did. She ran faster than she had at any other point in her life. Fueled by adrenaline and love. And fear.

Kate would die before she let these creatures get Veronica.

The shrieks drew closer. Her heart beat furiously. A sheen of sweat covered her brow. An incessant chattering haunted her from behind. She wondered why her pursuers hadn't attacked. If these things could take down coyotes and mountain lions, catching a human female carrying a thirty-five-pound child would be trivial. Yet they hadn't. Why?

A powerful gust swept over her from above, followed by an extremely close but diminishing shriek. Kate dove to the dirt, narrowly avoiding being snatched up by whatever had swooped over her.

Kate prepared for death. Perhaps these creatures were just toying with her—biding their time until they snatched her up. It had to be. In her mind, there was no other possible explanation.

And yet, she lifted Veronica back up on her shoulder and kept running. Kate scrambled for the campsite. She didn't run as fast—she couldn't. She'd burned up all that energy long ago. Yet run she did, fueled only by sheer will. By the resolve of a mother protecting her child.

More shrieks punctuated the hostile darkness. The insistent nattering and chattering crescendoed. The beasts skulking in the night tightened their pincer.

Before she realized it, Kate had emerged from the last wash before the campsite. By her estimation, she was within thirty feet of Danaher's police cruiser. With one final all-out burst of energy, she sprinted to her salvation.

When she reached the vehicle, she stumbled upon two bodies.

Danaher and Chambless. Their faces smeared with the purple secretion. Their noses and ears shorn from their heads.

Kate knew at that instant it was only a matter of time before she and Veronica were next. As if to underscore that thought, something swooped down from the sky and landed with a formidable thump behind her. Kate set Veronica on the ground and shielded her with her body, crouching over her daughter and wrapping her arms around her.

This is the end, Kate thought. She fortified herself for a last stand.

A rush of air swirled above her. A second creature touched down beside the first. Kate refused to turn, frightened it might provoke a reaction. She glanced down at Danaher and spotted the revolver in his hand.

The ground shook as a third creature landed in front of Kate. As the winged thing leered from just beyond the edge of the police cruiser's headlights, Kate could only glimpse fragments of it. A flash of a membranous wing. A wedge-shaped snout. Razor-sharp and finger-length fangs. The dim luminescence of otherworldly eyes. The guttural growls and chitters.

Kate was no biologist or linguist, but she was pretty sure these vocalizations bore the unmistakable signs of language.

The light behind her undulated in sympathy with the loud thud of a fourth beast landing on the police car's trunk. Keeping Veronica close, Kate slowly crouched toward Danaher. The creature in front of her squealed in protest. Kate shuddered as its foul mildew-like breath washed over her.

But it still hadn't attacked. Why?

At that precise moment, Kate knew what she had to do. She lurched toward Danaher's pistol. She grabbed it. The beast in front of her roared. Another wave of its fetid breath rolled over her. A breath that was not hot but cold.

Then, in all its alien horror, the creature stepped into the light. Veronica screamed.

It was massive, about nine feet from muzzle to tail. It had a saurian feel to it. Kate wouldn't have called it a dinosaur but could understand why others had made the comparison. But unlike any dinosaur in the fossil record, it had six appendages—four arms and two legs. Its overlong body reminded Kate of a praying mantis. She supposed it was required to support the extra set of arms. The underside of each arm and leg had a membranous wing, akin to a bat's. The six-winged abomination also had other curious, more alien features. Scattered throughout its pale white scales were mushroom-like purplish bulbs.

Sheltering Veronica beneath her body, Kate pointed the pistol at the monstrosity. It seemed to waver—as if it understood the threat. It hissed at Kate.

She kept the pistol trained on the cryptid. With a taloned finger on its three-fingered claw, it pointed at Veronica. Kate shuddered. That was it—the only reason these things hadn't slaughtered her. They wanted her little girl. And she'd be damned if she ever let them have her.

Kate shielded her daughter with even more of her body in the clearest nonverbal indication that she'd die before surrendering her child to these fiends.

A creature behind her chattered in clicks and pops. The one in front replied in kind, then hissed at her again. Without warning, it opened its jaws and sprayed purple venom at her like a cobra. By instinct, Kate lowered her head, narrowly averting the spray. She pointed the pistol at the creature and pulled the trigger in quick succession. Two shots hit the beast center-of-mass. It shrieked, stumbling backward. She turned to fire at the other three, but by the time she'd aimed her weapon, they'd all taken flight into the darkness, disappearing into the cold night.

Kate didn't waste any time. She jumped to her feet, lifted Veronica back onto her shoulder, and sprinted to her car. She got in and drove until she nearly ran out of gas. She refueled in Bakersfield, then kept going all the way back to Pasadena. But she didn't sleep—she couldn't sleep. For the Lone Pine Mountain Devils would haunt her memories until the end of her days.

When Kate woke, she would have said there was a man in her bedroom, but it technically wasn't a man. It was a silhouette shaped like one.

"Do not scream," the simulacrum said in a modulated voice.

As she stared at the dark form standing at the foot of her bed, she was reminded of the episode her father had done on the shadow people—horrifying nocturnal visitors flickering on the edge of one's vision. The apparitions often paralyzed their victims, sometimes attempting to suffocate or choke them. She couldn't remember what her father had uncovered about the phenomenon, but the thought that this being might be one of them terrified her. And yet, there was something more tangible about this night visitor that allowed her to discount this initial impression. She slowed her breathing to calm herself.

"Who are you?" she asked.

"That doesn't matter," he replied. "What does matter is that I mean you no harm."

Kate shivered with fear. She bit her lip to wake up from the dream, only to confirm it wasn't one. "Then why didn't you just knock on my door like a normal person? You committed a felony by breaking into my apartment."

The figure shrugged. "Technically, I never broke into your apartment. I'm not here physically. What you see is a projection."

The reptilian rump of her brain urged her to flee. Her mind conjured a myriad of frightful possibilities. She exhaled to center herself. *Stay calm.* "I see. So *how* am I seeing a projection in my apartment in the middle of the night? And while we're at it, why?"

The figure nodded. "I was just about to get to that point. The incident at Lone Pine. My organization needs to formally debrief you. We can't have civilians wandering around with the knowledge you possess."

"So, you're from the government?" Kate said.

"I'm sorry. I can't discuss any of that right now."

"Okay. Then what can you discuss?"

"Tomorrow morning, you will find an envelope under your door at precisely 7 A.M. Ensure you retrieve it immediately. It is imperative no one else has an opportunity to intercept it. Even now, others could be listening in on our conversation. To reduce the risk of interception, you need to be waiting for the package to arrive and retrieve it instantly."

Kate scratched her head. "And if I don't?"

"I highly recommend you don't pursue that path. Refusal is not an option." The man's voice paused as if to let his veiled threat linger like a haunted soul in an abandoned mine.

"And what will this package contain?" Kate said, letting the words out in carefully modulated packets of her own fear, lest it erupt in an uncontrolled rout.

"Further instructions." the modulated voice replied.

"Why should I trust you?"

"A most excellent question, Dr. Weaver. Someone you trust will call you after you retrieve and review the instructions. They will give you the comfort you need."

"I see."

With that, the black silhouette shimmered and vanished. Kate stared at the dark wall and once again wondered what the hell kind of a sordid mess she'd gotten herself into.

The next morning at precisely 7:00 A.M., a manila envelope slid beneath Kate's door. With trepidation, she grabbed it and tore it open, unfolding a slip of paper inside. On the letter, there were a date, a time, and an address. The date was today's; the time was 10:00 A.M.; the location was a building on Caltech's campus that Kate had never visited. It gave her just enough time to drop Veronica off at school and get to the meeting with some buffer. She didn't know whether to appreciate the careful consideration of her schedule or to be horrified someone had known her daily routine well enough to organize a meeting around it.

Trip Dorn called at precisely 7:01 A.M.

"You need to trust these people," Trip said. "I've been working with them for the better part of a decade, and they've never once let me down. Over time, you'll come to know and respect them. They have the country's best interests in mind. More importantly, they are watching out for humanity's best interests."

"Thanks for the reassurance, Trip, but I need to know who these people are. And why are they slipping envelopes under my door?"

"I'm sorry, Kate. I can't answer that question right now. You never know who could be monitoring our conversation."

"Like who? The Chinese?" she said.

"I only wish it was the Chinese," Trip replied, "but there are far more sinister forces out there. Hell, seventy percent of the time, we're working with the Chinese. There are things out there that threaten every nation. Threats you couldn't possibly imagine."

"Such as?"

"I'm sorry, Kate, but I'm going to have to cut our conversation short. Just promise me you'll trust these people."

Kate hesitated.

"Promise me," Trip insisted.

She sighed. "Fine, Trip. I'll consider it."

"Good," he said. "You won't regret it."

After she ended her call, Kate read the instructions again, unsure what she should do. But she reminded herself of Trip's assurances. And Trip was a man she trusted implicitly. So, she got Veronica ready for the day, dropped her off at school, then headed to Caltech.

Kate walked down an empty hallway in a sealed-off wing of an otherwise deserted one-story sandstone building hidden among other unremarkable sandstone buildings. Kate took a deep breath before she entered the designated room. As she walked in, three men waited at the end of an oak boardroom table. Two had crewcuts and wore starched black suits with white shirts and black ties. The third man was bald, overweight, and had a disheveled beard dusted with what appeared to be the sprinkles from a white powdered donut. The open box of Dunkin'

Donuts at the center of the table only heightened her suspicion that he was Dr. Eli Rosen.

One of the men in black extended his hand toward a chair on the left side of the table and said, "Good morning, Dr. Weaver. Please close the door behind you and have a seat."

The man's bearing and command presence gave Kate the distinct impression he was or had been in the military. She also didn't appreciate being ordered around by someone she didn't know and whose authority she didn't recognize. Kate shut the door but refused to sit.

"I'm sorry, but I'd prefer to stand," she said.

The man glowered at her for several uncomfortable seconds, apparently unaccustomed to being challenged.

Something about the bald man seemed familiar, but Kate couldn't quite place him. Regardless, she decided to seize the initiative and go on the offensive. "And you are?"

"I'm asking the questions here," the man said.

"My apologies," the bald man intervened. "My colleague here has forgotten his manners. Would you like a donut?"

Kate looked at him expectantly.

The man dusted off his powder-covered hands, walked over to Kate, and offered his hand. "Again, my apologies. I'm Dr. Eli Rosen. We had a phone conversation a few days ago. I'm glad to see you healthy and well."

Kate greatly relaxed upon finally meeting Rosen in person. Whatever happened in this room, she was at least confident she had an ally here. "It's a pleasure to finally meet you, Dr. Rosen. Now, can someone tell me why you put me through all this cloak and dagger stuff?"

"Happy to," Rosen said. "And please, call me, Eli. Now, let me introduce you to my colleagues. I think we all may have gotten started on the wrong foot."

"We most certainly did," Kate said.

Rosen motioned toward the man who'd challenged Kate. "This is Howard Lasseter. He works with me at... ah... the organization we work for. Sorry, I can't really disclose what that is just yet, but please bear with me. We have a lot to go through with you today. Once we do that, it will become more apparent why we are a little reticent to share details. Though, I promise that over time, more will be revealed to you."

"Yeah, yeah," Kate said, "that's what they keep telling me." She walked around the table and shook Lasseter's hand.

Gesturing toward the second man, Rosen said, "This is Juan Perez."

"Nice to meet you, Juan," said Kate to the pastiest white man she'd ever encountered.

"Likewise," Juan said.

"Those aren't your real names, are they?" Kate said.

Juan smiled and nudged Lasseter. "This one catches on quick, doesn't she?"

Lasseter frowned and shrugged with a light growl.

"All right, gentlemen," Kate said. "Now that we're done with all the... *pleasantries*, can someone please tell me why I'm here?"

Lasseter straightened with such confidence that Kate was certain he was anxious to reassert his authority. "Dr. Weaver, you were involved in a highly peculiar incident last evening. Soon, very soon, reporters will begin hounding you. That is, if they haven't already. Moreover, you never alerted authorities to the second massacre. You fled straight back to Pasadena without telling a soul."

Kate rubbed her eyes. She was exhausted. The man had a point. She really should've called the police, but her drive to keep her daughter safe had overridden every other impulse. And even if she had alerted the authorities, what the hell would she have said? What the hell would *they* have done?

"If you're here to arrest me, just cut the shit and arrest me," Kate said, tired of Lasseter's bullshit.

Rosen held out his hands in a calming motion. "No one is going to arrest you, Dr. Weaver. In fact, you're a hero. All of us see you in that light. And your discretion in keeping the matter... quiet is something we all very much appreciate." He looked over his shoulder at Lasseter.

Lasseter gave a curt nod in what Kate could only describe as begrudging.

"What Howard is trying to get at is that we will help you manage through this process. This debriefing is just the first step. Our goal today is to get your take on exactly what happened, so we can contain any blowback."

"I see," Kate said. "Why didn't you say that in the first place?"

Rosen grinned and shrugged.

After Kate had finished recounting everything she could remember from the instant she'd learned of her father's disappearance until the moment she'd returned to Pasadena, the conversation quickly shifted to the speculative.

"So, based on your experience," Rosen said, "what do you believe the Lone Pine Mountain Devils actually are?"

Kate perked up at this question. Now the discussion was starting to get interesting.

"Well, I'm not really an expert on cryptozoology, or even biology, for that matter..." she said.

"Ah, but that's where you're wrong," Rosen replied. "That's where you're selling yourself short, Kate. You're a scientist. And like all scientists, you bring a unique perspective to the table that most other folks might not. Indulge us."

"Well, if I had to speculate, I'd say the creatures are sentient lifeforms from either another world or dimension. Their species seems to be some combination of reptile and fungi. Their feeding or reproductive cycle involves the spread of a purplish mucous that contains thousands of spores. Based on local seismic activity in Lone Pine and my review of the historical record, their appearance coincides with the emission of point source gravitational waves. My hypothesis, were I to formulate one, would be that these waves are associated with the opening of a wormhole in space-time that connects their world with ours. In fact, based on oral histories and myths passed down by the Paiute people, I'd say these cryptids have been visiting Earth for millennia."

"Very cogent analysis, Kate," Rosen said. "What else?"

"That's everything I can think of," Kate answered. "No, wait. I had visited a local Paiute man named Dr. Henry Black to see if the Lone Pine Mountain Devil had featured in Paiute myth and legend. In response, he told me an old tale of a trapper who ensnared a coyote. The coyote spoke to him. It warned him not to trap other coyotes or skin them. This coyote had also been combing the universe for a missing star. The coyote warned of a division in the universe that it would reveal in the future."

"And what was the point of this story about a coyote that wasn't a coyote?" Rosen said.

"I have no idea," Kate replied. "I can only venture a wild guess."

"Go ahead. We won't hold it against you."

"Maybe the coyote was somehow under the influence of this purple substance. Like my father was."

"Bingo!" Rosen shouted. He seemed almost too excited for Kate's taste.

He grabbed another donut—a Boston Kreme—and took a bite. His mouth full, he continued to speak. "Are you familiar with *Hymenoepimecis argyraphaga*?"

"What?" Kate said.

"*Hymenoepimecis argyraphaga* is a Costa Rican wasp that has a parasitic relationship with the spider, *Plesiometa argyra*. You see, this wasp temporarily paralyzes the spider with the venom from its sting and then lays eggs on the spider's abdomen, replacing the spider's own eggs if any are present. When the eggs hatch, the wasp larvae inject a chemical into the spider that triggers it to build a web whose design is unlike anything the spider normally constructs—a web the spider has never before spun in its entire short life. The web's function is to serve as a cocoon that protects a wasp larva while it pupates. Once this web cocoon is complete, the wasp larva kills the spider, pupates, and ultimately emerges from the cocoon as an adult wasp. Then the cycle begins anew."

Dumbfounded, Kate asked, "Why are you telling me this?"

"Tell me about your father," Rosen said. "What do you recall the last time you saw him?"

"His eyes," she said. "Those terrible purple eyes. He seemed to be completely under their spell. He was so far gone, I had to abandon him." Kate wiped a tear from her cheek. "I didn't want to leave him behind. God, I didn't. But I had no choice. It was either him or Veronica. And he was so far gone."

Rosen walked up to Kate and hugged her. Kate wasn't the touchy-feely type, but Rosen's act of compassion nearly made her crumble. He didn't have to do this; he didn't have to show he cared. But he did it anyway.

"You did the right thing," he said, patting her back. "There's nothing else you could have done. Don't blame yourself."

Rosen waited for Kate to calm down. To get ahold of herself. She was embarrassed by her display of emotion, but she figured, under the circumstances, it was understandable.

Rosen surprised her with another question: "Have you ever asked yourself why your father hadn't been ravaged? Why he still had ears and a nose?"

Kate looked up at Rosen. "How did you know that?"

"Answer my question," he said.

"Maybe the spores in the purple secretion have a different effect on different people and animals?" she answered.

"Bingo, again," Rosen said, appearing oddly proud of her. "Our working theory is that the spores sicken ninety-plus percent of the organisms they infect. When the spores don't take, the Lone Pine Mountain Devil entities maul the infected. But for the rare organisms in which the spores do take root, the entities hijack their prey's higher executive functions. In this particular case, they were able to influence your father to steal your daughter much like the wasp controls the spider."

"Jesus," was all Kate could muster in response. Then a deeper, far darker realization swept over her. "Why... why did they want him to take Veronica?"

Suddenly, Kate remembered Dr. Black's odd fixation on her daughter—the creepy comments about shamans.

"Oh, my God," she said out loud before she could stop herself.

"What is it, Kate?" Rosen said.

"Dr. Black warned me. He told me he sensed some sort of shamanic power in Veronica. Told me to protect her for others would sense it too. I thought he was a crackpot. Maybe. Just maybe he wasn't. Maybe there was something to it."

"There is something to it," Lasseter piped up.

Kate shuddered.

Lasseter continued, "We just don't know what it is yet."

Then a horrifying thought popped into Kate's head. "Was... was Veronica... infected?"

Kate braced herself for the answer, expecting a devastating conclusion.

"We don't believe so," Lasseter replied.

"How can you be so sure?"

Rosen placed his hand on her shoulder in a reassuring manner. "We'll confirm with a lab test, but Veronica's showing none of the tell-tale signs of infection."

"Which are?"

"Lethargy, confusion, discoloration of the eyes to start," Rosen answered.

Kate thought back to the point when she had dropped Veronica off at school. She tried to remember every detail about her daughter's behavior and appearance. She didn't think Veronica had looked or acted in any way out of the ordinary, but Kate could never really be too sure. And being a mother only exacerbated her paranoia.

"I guess she hasn't been showing any of those symptoms," Kate said. "How do you know the spores aren't just dormant like anthrax. Can't anthrax spores be reactivated after lying dormant for decades? How can you be sure these spores don't do the same thing?"

"Well, first off, anthrax is a bacillus," Rosen said. "These cryptids are animal-fungi hybrids. We've found nothing in our research to indicate these spores survive very long outside their hosts' bodies."

Kate paused as she had another disquieting thought. "Wait, how would you know what my daughter's symptoms are?"

Without skipping a beat or showing any sense of embarrassment or shame, Lasseter replied, "Because our organization has been surveilling you since you arrived in Lone Pine. And we stand by our current assessment."

Kate felt violated. "Is… is that even legal?"

Rosen smiled. "Let's just say we're part of a special organization with special powers. But don't worry, we have your best interests at heart."

Rosen's words didn't do much to reassure her. All she could think about was who was watching these watchers? Who was responsible for their oversight? Hell, who did they even represent? For all she knew, they might not even be American agents. What if they were Russian or Chinese operatives? If they were, the act of merely cooperating with them would make her guilty of espionage.

"When are you all going to reveal who you work for?" Kate said. "I'm not comfortable talking or working with an organization I don't know."

"Did your Nobel-Prize-winning colleague not vouch for our organization?" Lasseter said.

"Well, yes."

"Do you really think someone who'd won the Nobel Prize would stick their neck out for a nefarious organization?" Lasseter continued. "Especially one you know and trust?"

"Didn't Yasser Arafat vouch for the PLO?"

Lasseter scowled.

Kate continued. "You still didn't answer my question."

Rosen looked over at Lasseter as if asking for permission. Lasseter stared back, seemingly in thought. After a long pause, Lasseter nodded. Rosen nodded back and faced Kate. "Right now, we're in the process of conducting a fairly significant background check on you. It is much more comprehensive than a typical clearance investigation. Once you're fully vetted, we'll share more details with you about our organization. Until then, you're going to have to trust us, and we understand that trust doesn't come cheap. For your time here, we've already deposited fifty-thousand dollars in your bank account as a retainer. You've already provided the services for that amount. Once your background check clears, you'll be issued a security clearance. At that point, we'll reveal more about our organization."

The sudden and large cash infusion in her account certainly did nothing to reassure her. In fact, it had the opposite effect—it made her even more paranoid. She tried to focus her mind on other things. "What of the creatures in Lone Pine? What do you intend to do about them?"

Lasseter smiled for the first time Kate had known him. "The infestation has been neutralized."

"What does that even mean?" Kate said. "Did you send troops to wipe them out? Did you infect them with a virus? Did you close the wormhole?"

Lasseter's jaws clamped shut as he murdered his uncharacteristic grin. "I'm sorry, Dr. Weaver, that's classified."

Because of course it was, she thought. The key question now was: by whom? Kate resigned herself to the fact that she'd have to wait for the answer. And that required patience, but Kate was not a patient woman. Yet she let it pass, for there was one question she'd been dreading to ask all meeting. Now was the time to do it.

"What about my father? Have you found his... body?"

The men shot nervous glances at each other, but no one seemed to have the guts to respond.

After several uncomfortable seconds of silence, Rosen said, "I'm sorry, Kate. We haven't been able to recover his body. And to be honest, we still don't know if he's alive or dead."

"But the infection. He's still infected, isn't he?" she said, a slight ring of hope in her voice.

"If he's still alive, he's still infected," Lasseter said. "And based on our knowledge of the spores, his mental faculties have likely experienced significant degradation. If we were to find him today, there's very little we'd be able to do for him. The infection is similar to the rabies virus. If you act quickly, there may be time to save someone. If you don't, there's no hope."

"I see," Kate said. "What about the others? All those people in their campers that the Lone Pine Mountain Devils slaughtered? What about Sheriff Danaher and Deputy Chambless?"

"We've also sanitized the crime scene. A few days from now, hikers will stumble upon the bodies along the Pacific Crest Trail. It will feed into the Lone Pine Mountain Devil legend, but people will never know the full extent of the interdimensional breach. Nor should they ever know."

"So, you're organizing a cover-up."

Lasseter tightened his jawed, obviously holding in a torrent of rage. "We're doing what we must to avoid panicking the population. Most importantly, we'd very much appreciate your cooperation in this matter, Dr. Weaver. Not a word to anyone about anything that transpired on the night you witnessed the wormhole's opening."

"Or what?"

Rosen patted her on the shoulder. "Please, Kate. Be smart. You can talk about anything before that night, but everything about that night in particular is classified." He looked over his shoulder at Lasseter, then faced Kate again. "These people don't do nuance well. They are also the best in the world at making problems disappear. Understand?"

Kate hated when people even hinted at trying to intimidate her, but she trusted Rosen. She knew his intentions came from a good place. She nodded. "Understood." She looked back at Lasseter. "This isn't the first time you've covered up something like this, is it?"

True to form, Lasseter responded with a succinct, "That's classified."

She decided to let it go. "So, what's next?"

"You go about your life as you otherwise would have," Rosen said. "When the investigation is complete, we'll contact you."

As if her experiences at Lone Pine weren't enough, Kate wondered how deep this cryptid conspiracy might go, who might be involved, and how extensive their reach was. Kate shook every-one's hands then left the building. She kept her head on a swivel. She knew they'd be shadowing her from here on forward, but it still didn't mean she shouldn't watch her back. If she spotted someone, she knew there was nothing she could do, of course. But at least she'd have the satisfaction of thwarting the bastards.

The celebration of Mack Gavin's life was an overstated affair replete with both serious media and disgusting paparazzi. De-spite the stark differences in their outward appearances, Kate wondered: was there really any difference? Both flavors harassed you. The paparazzi did it when they went after the story; more respectable media did it by publishing lies masquerading as truth.

In the days leading up to Mack Gavin's funeral, the media had been merciless on Kate. At various points, she'd been described as a sex-starved divorcee vixen. Men she'd never met had come forward to claim sexual liaisons she'd never had. Even Harrison Robbins at CNN, who had singlehandedly crafted her father's hagiography, had turned against her. He'd begun one report with: "Dr. Kate Gavin Weaver. Mother. Daughter. Astrophysicist. The apple couldn't have fallen farther from the tree."

She took it all in stride. She focused on what was important, and that was saying goodbye to her father. But that was kind of hard to do when white gangster rapper, Grande Allah Mowed, recited a lyrical rap at the celebration about how her father was "Cool with the Crips 'Cause He's Down with the Cryptids." Especially when it was inside a Catholic church.

Because they'd never found a body, Kate's mother had held a celebration for Mack the night before the funeral in lieu of a wake. This decision, of course, led to the melding of strange bedfellows. But Kate knew it was just a casualty of her father's stardom.

For several days before the celebration, Kate had wrestled with the decision to deliver her father's eulogy. But she'd ulti-mately come to the conclusion that it was critical for closure. There were things she'd never had the chance to say to her father during his life—things she'd never have the opportunity to say again. As far as she was concerned, this ritual of death was the last opportunity she'd ever have to make peace with her father.

As her time to deliver the eulogy drew closer, Kate found herself wiping sweat off her face. Her heart quickened in anticipation. At times she felt lightheaded and nauseated. Kate had never had an issue speaking before large crowds, but those speeches had nearly always involved presenting extremely technical content to an audience filled with highly intelligent and educated people. For the most part, this crowd was the opposite.

When her appointed time came, Kate stood up, straightened her black dress, and calmly approached the podium positioned in front of the altar. She pulled out a wadded slip of paper, unfolded it, and then laid it onto the podium. She took a deep, calming breath.

"As you all know, my father sent me to Catholic school. When I was six, the nuns would have us memorize the answers to the Baltimore Catechism. At the end of his long day, he'd help me memorize the answers to questions such as: Who made the world, and who is God?

"Once, one particular question inspired him to ask me another. The question was: why did God make you? As a very young Catholic schoolgirl, I dutifully responded, 'God made me to know Him, to love Him, and to serve Him in this world, so that I can be happy with Him forever in Heaven.' There was something about the specificity and certainty of my rote answer that rankled him because his next question went way off-script. He looked me dead in the eye and said, 'How do you know that's true?'

"That single question shattered my world. I responded, 'Because Sister George told me so.'

"Relentless, he pressed further. 'How do you know Sister George is right?'

"The six-year-old me didn't have an answer. Hell, the thirty-eight-year-old me still doesn't. But that wasn't the point of my father's question. His point was epistemological." Kate paused as she surveyed the crowd to observe a preponderance of confused expressions. Given the overrepresentation of Hollywood and media types, this was to be expected. She smiled and continued. "His point was about the fundamental nature of knowledge. How can we truly know what is real? This single powerful question shaped my life from that point forward. A life dedicated to seeking out the truth no matter what I found or where I found it. A life that at once was both enriching and devastating. A life unvarnished by pretense or illusion. A life chiseled down to the cold reality of matter and energy.

"This push to question the fundamental nature of reality was a gift and... a curse. It led to everything I've ever accomplished as an astrophysicist but also led to a failed marriage. A relentless focus on the truth can be an albatross in the realm of human affairs. Sometimes, it's best that we ignore it."

Kate paused. She let her words linger. She knew her sentiments had an especially relevant and powerful resonance for the people in the audience representing the entertainment and media industries. They, of all people, trafficked more than most in illusion and deceit.

"When my father decided to give up a decent and stable life as an evolutionary biologist to enter the speculative field of cryptozoology, my mother nearly lost her mind. The first few years were the hardest on my family. Supported by what was effectively a single income from my mother's job as a nurse, we really struggled. And it often looked like we weren't going to make it to the next paycheck. But my father was stubborn. He never gave up his dreams. He doggedly pursued the truth no matter where it led.

"It's hard to fault him for ruthlessly adhering to his principles. Like most 'overnight successes,'" Kate said, accentuating her point with finger quotes, "my dad's ten-year struggle finally led to his seminal cryptozoological documentary on the Dark Watchers of Big Sur."

The crowd roared in laughter at Kate's inside joke.

"After years of struggle, his life—and ours—turned around with *The Cryptid Hunter's* monumental success. Suddenly, we were no longer living from paycheck to paycheck. My father could finally afford to send my brother, Chas, and me to college. For once in our lives, we wanted for nothing.

"And yet the hairline fractures and fault lines remained, hidden beneath the gilded veneer of my father's success. My rigorous drive for the truth inspired by my father led to conflict with the same man. As I went off to Stanford to study physics, I found myself ashamed by my father's elevation of what I'd believed to be pseudoscience. I saw his embrace of cryptozoology as a betrayal to the principles he'd instilled in that impressionable six-year-old girl.

"Over the years, this tear in our relationship widened into a yawning chasm. We'd reached an impasse. We were both so stubborn neither of us spoke to one another for several years."

Kate hesitated. She tightened her jaw to stifle her roiling emotions. She wiped eyes pregnant with tears. She continued. "My father's disappearance changed all that. It's funny how a crisis can wash away all the muddy emotional baggage from the bedrock of an enduring relationship. But more importantly, so can truth.

"As I spent the last week searching for my father, I've learned things that have challenged my longest and strongest held biases. My father's disappearance opened my eyes up to a world that not only reinforced my understanding of gravitational waves but also connected my life's work to my father's. Everything is connected. But you'll never see it if you don't open your mind to the possibilities."

A lump formed in Kate's throat. She wiped her eyes again. "I love my father. I will always love him. While my relationship was much more turbulent than the one he had with his adoring fans, it was also much deeper and richer. Running my father's gauntlet helped make me the woman I am today. It made me a better scientist, a better mother, and a better human being. I will always cherish my father's memory, and I trust you all will too. Thank you, and God bless you all."

As Kate walked away from the podium, the crowd erupted. Waves of bittersweet sorrow and sympathy seemed to sweep through the audience and wash over Kate. So powerful were these feelings, they seemed almost tangible. So powerful, she struggled to contain the emotion that threatened to burst from inside her.

If somewhere her father had been looking down upon her, he would have been proud. She was sure of it.

At the end of the event, as the guests funneled their way out of the church, a dapper and wiry man with close-cropped gray hair waltzed up to the front row pews where Kate had been sitting. She recognized him but couldn't quite place who he was.

"Kate," he said, exuding an unshakable air of confidence. "Your eulogy was absolutely breathtaking. I never knew you had such passion and sentimentality hiding inside you. I don't mean to insult you. You've always struck me as a bit of a grind. No offense. But that speech. Wow. Just wow."

"I'm not really sure how I should take that, but thanks?" Kate said. Then she remembered. The party at her father's mansion. It was Logan Rhys-Barrington, the producer of *The Cryptid Hunter*.

"No, really," he insisted. "You have a lot of untapped talent."

Kate really didn't know how to take the compliment. Was Logan hitting on her? Honestly, with everything written in the tabloids and mainstream media, she wouldn't have doubted it. "Okay," she said, inviting him to say more.

He handed her his business card. "Call me early next week. I have a proposal for you."

Kate accepted the card. "Will do."

After everyone left, Kate lingered. She thought about her father and his influence on her life. For the first time in years, Kate broke down and cried.

Over the next several weeks, Kate did her best to settle back into her daily routine. The media continued to harass her in the days following her father's funeral, but like gnats discovering a hemorrhaging goat, their attention quickly shifted to bloodier flavors. That was a good thing. She was already concerned the press's aggressive onslaught on her reputation might have been fatal in her quest for tenure. It wasn't until she received the ominous call from Dr. Dorn that she'd finally know for sure.

"Kate," he said. "I have some discouraging news."

"I didn't get tenure, did I?" she said.

"Not this year," he said reassuringly, "but there's always next year."

She couldn't believe those semi-literate parasites had done her in. She'd always believed that the academic community would easily see through all the bullshit. Apparently not. "I guess my father picked the wrong year to die," she said.

"Why on Earth would you say something so terrible?" Dorn said, his voice tinged with a patina of disgust.

"Well, without all the media attention, I figured I would have been a shoo-in."

Dorn chuckled. "Hell, Kate, the media attention was one of the strongest aspects of your candidacy. You are one of the most effective communicators I know. God knows we need more people like you to market the hard sciences."

"If it wasn't all the negative media attention, what stopped me from getting tenure this year?"

"Well, as a member of the Tenure Committee, it would be highly irregular for me to comment on those specifics," he said.

"Trip, how long have I known you?"

"Your entire stint at Caltech. What's that, seven years?"

"Exactly," Kate replied. "We've worked together on several groundbreaking projects. I can tell from your voice that you're disappointed with the Tenure Committee's decision. You at least owe me a hint of why it happened. Because, frankly, I don't want to be one of those adjunct professors who haunts a university campus forever hoping to get tenure someday soon, when there's something in their file that renders that dream impossible."

She heard him sigh. "I see your point. Let's just say there was a complaint about your behavior. A recent complaint."

"Let me guess," she said, "it happened around the time my father went missing."

"I'm sorry, Kate. I can't say anymore."

"I understand. I appreciate your candor. This university doesn't deserve you, Trip."

"It doesn't deserve you either, Kate."

"Level with me, Trip," she said. "If I stay, will I ever make tenure at Caltech?"

There was a long, uncomfortable silence. "I'm sorry, Kate, but you'll never make tenure. If you decide to go to another university, I will always support you. You're the finest astrophysicist I've ever had the pleasure of knowing. Unfortunately, politics trumps competence in our line of work."

"Thanks, Trip. I appreciate the endorsement. I'm sure our paths will cross again."

Trip laughed. "I'm counting on it."

After Kate ended her call, she just shook her head. She reflected on Trip's final words about politics and competence and knew right then and there that Dr. Carley Cabrillo had almost certainly sabotaged her file with a complaint. Kate wanted to smash a window, but lashing out would do her no good. She simply had to move on. At least she still had Veronica.

As it turned out, Kate's father hadn't forgotten her or Veronica in his will. In the next week, she'd be receiving enough money for her to never have to work another day for the rest of her life. It wasn't in Kate's DNA to stop working, but it sure as hell wasn't in her nature to stay in the rat race when she didn't need to.

Kate spent the next hour composing her letter of resignation, then fired it off in an email to the university. After that, she never looked back.

As strange as it may have sounded, Kate found it cathartic to be back in Lone Pine. After she'd resigned from Caltech, she'd pulled out Logan Rhys-Barrington's card and had decided to call him. To her surprise, he'd offered her her father's job as host of *The Cryptid Hunter*.

Initially, she'd struggled with the decision. On the one hand, she had been concerned that hosting the show would forever tarnish her professional reputation. On the other hand, her experience in Lone Pine had opened her mind to the prospect that there were still very real physical phenomena that scientists had not yet examined because of the damage it might do to their careers. And unlike her father, she had felt she could bring more scientific rigor to the process.

Once she'd made up her mind, she'd never looked back.

Now, here she was on site, filming the show's tenth-anniversary episode and honoring her father's not inconsiderable contributions to the cryptozoological field.

To make sure she didn't run afoul of the powers that be, she'd nominally hired Dr. Eli Rosen as a consultant for the show. But his real purpose was to provide his organization with comfort that Kate would keep a lid on the wormhole's existence. But Rosen had always been an easygoing and free-spirited man, so his presence was never an issue.

After Kate had finished filming a segment in the Alabama Hills, she sat down for a quick lunch with Rosen.

"You know," she said to him, "I very much enjoy our ongoing collaboration. I was kind of hoping this consulting arrangement would turn into a full-time gig for you. Your knowledge of fringe physics is unparalleled. And also, your other job kind of gives you a leg up on getting leads for future cryptid episodes. You interested?"

"Excuse me," a shrill voice announced from one of the talent trailers.

Kate rolled her eyes and chuckled.

Rosen's face registered an expression of confusion.

"Excuse me," the voice repeated. Dr. Carley Cabrillo was addressing some hapless key grip on the set. "My contract explicitly says, "still water, not sparkling. Yet every day this week, you people keep making the same mistake."

"It's not a mistake," Kate mumbled under her breath.

"You know," Rosen said, "I never quite figured out why you insist on keeping that woman on set. Any chance you can enlighten me?"

"What? The great Eli Rosen hasn't cracked the case yet?" Kate teased.

"Contrary to popular opinion, I'm not exactly Sherlock Holmes."

"Aren't your people doing an in-depth background investigation on me?" she said.

"Well, sure, but I'm not the guy who does it, and they keep the results classified."

"All right, fine," Kate said, "but you cannot tell a soul."

"Deal."

"You know how someone had sabotaged my career at Caltech?"

"That's her?" Rosen said.

"Yup," Kate said with a self-satisfied smirk.

Rosen's face reddened with apoplectic rage. "Well then, why the hell would you invite her to be on the show with you?"

Kate began to regret revealing her secret to Rosen. She'd never seen him react so strongly to anything in her life. He was normally so calm and low drama.

"Because I needed a geologist for this show," said Kate in the best deadpan expression she could muster.

"You couldn't find a better geologist?"

"Nope. There was only one geologist in the world who would do, and it was Dr. Carley Cabrillo, Caltech Professor of Geology and Geochemistry."

A look of realization appeared on Rosen's face. "You're going to publicly humiliate her on your show. That's genius."

Kate shook her head. "Eli, I'm not that stupid. If I did that, I'd put this show at risk by putting Caltech's reputation at risk."

"What's your game then?" Rosen asked.

"Well...," Kate began.

"Kate," Dr. Cabrillo's banshee wail interrupted. The woman lumbered toward Kate and Rosen like a hungry hippo. "I've been looking for you all morning. My schedule today just won't do. I've already been to the mine five times in the last two days. The crew keeps on insisting that we do more takes of my segment."

"Carley, you do realize that my show has thirty million weekly viewers, right?"

"And?" Carley said impatiently.

"You only have one chance to make a first impression. Don't you want to make sure your segment is the very best it can be?"

"Now that you put it that way, yes."

"Well, then buck up and get it done. Show us what it takes to get tenured at Caltech."

Carley hesitated for a moment. For a barely perceptible instant, her face betrayed a mix of irritation and consternation, then her mask returned. "Yes, I suppose so. Thank you for watching out for me."

"Good luck today, Carley," Kate said as the woman shambled back toward her trailer.

"That footage is never going to see the light of day," Kate said to Rosen.

Rosen laughed so hard, he fell out of his chair.

After the production team wrapped up filming on *The Cryptid Hunter*'s tenth episode, Kate heard a knock on her trailer door. She opened it to find Rosen standing there.

Kate smiled. "Come on in, Eli. Have a drink with me."

He entered the trailer and sat down. Kate grabbed a bottle of Johnny Walker Blue and poured herself a shot. She gestured toward the bottle to offer him a drink.

He held up his hand. "No, thanks. What I have to say should be fairly brief."

Disappointed, all Kate could come up with was, "Oh."

"I wanted to let you know that your investigation is complete."

"Should I be worried?" she said.

Rosen grinned. "Absolutely not. Your background check cleared with flying colors."

"Uh… good. And why's that significant?"

"Because you now have a TS/SCI clearance."

"And I'd need a top-secret clearance because?" she replied.

"Remember a few days ago when you offered me a full-time job?"

"Yes."

"Well, now I'm offering you one," he said.

"Stop right there," Kate said. "I already have a job; a job I've come to love."

Rosen smiled. "I thought you'd say that. What if I were to tell you that you can still do this job and the job I'm offering. Not only that. The job I'm offering you will help you do this job better."

Now Rosen had Kate's attention. "Go on," she said.

"As I promised a few weeks ago," Rosen said, "once we completed your background check, I'd be able to tell you more about my organization."

"So, tell me about it."

"It's codenamed Project CERBERUS. It's a classified organization housed in the Department of Defense that investigates and responds to extraterrestrial, extradimensional, and paranormal threats to both the United States and the world."

"And the acronym, CERBERUS, stands for?"

"Cosmic Entity Rapid Breach Envelopment and Ultra-containment Syndicate."

"Well, that's certainly a mouthful." Kate ran her fingers through her hair. "I'm definitely intrigued by the idea, but what the hell do I have to offer? I'm just a scientist."

"We always need more scientists, especially more of your caliber."

"Won't it interfere with my current job?"

"Don't worry. We can offer a very flexible arrangement and contract on an assignment basis. When you aren't filming, your job will offer about three months or so of downtime. We'll only assign you to cases during that period."

"What if a case stretches into something longer?" she said.

"Then another agent or your partner will pick it up until you're able to return to it."

"I see. And who's my partner?"

Rosen grinned. "You're looking at him."

Kate smiled back. "Was the Lone Pine Mountain Devil incident typical of these cases?"

Shaking his head, Rosen said, "Oh goodness, no. Most cases are much milder... and safer. What you experienced with the Lone Pine Mountain Devil was probably as dangerous as it's ever gonna get."

Kate was definitely interested. And the role would certainly complement what she was doing with her show. At the moment, she had no method for sourcing new material other than scouring threads on Reddit to learn about recent cryptid sightings or discover new ones. By accepting this position, she'd probably reduce the amount of time she had to work.

"And the pay and benefits?" she asked.

"Gold-plated."

Kate took a moment to consider the offer. "Well, all right. Pending all the fine print, I'm in."

"Excellent! I'm glad you accepted the job so quickly. Your first case starts tomorrow."

"Wait... what?" Kate said, dumbfounded.

"It's a rescue operation right here in Lone Pine."

"A... rescue... operation. I'm hardly trained for such things," Kate said.

Rosen gestured toward his massive belly. "If I can do it, you can too."

Kate had no logical retort. "Fair point."

"And just who is it we're rescuing?"

Rosen smiled. "Mack Gavin."

EPILOGUE

TEN YEARS LATER...

The brutal cold of an Andover winter had a sinister way of creeping into a girl's bones and slowly leaching out the heat. Veronica had just turned fourteen and was having trouble adjusting to the misery of a Massachusetts winter. She sorely missed her mother but knew that attending a prestigious boarding school would put her on the right path in life.

There was something about the cold that made Veronica feel bloated. She also often heard a faint humming that reminded her of discordant wind chimes in a snowstorm. Whenever she'd mentioned this to her roommate, she'd look at Veronica as if she had an elephant tusk sprouting from her forehead. For the first several weeks of November, the feeling was manageable, but as the days got progressively colder and stretched into late December, Veronica began to suspect something was deeply wrong.

The week before Christmas, after Veronica's roommate had already left for the holiday season, Veronica woke in the middle of the night. An intense pressure was building in her stomach. A pain so deep, she was sure she was going to die.

Falling out of her bed, she stumbled toward the doorway. Nauseated, she struggled to hold it in until she fumbled down the hallway and into the dorm's bathroom.

The pressure kept building, but nothing came out. Veronica dry-heaved into the toilet bowl, begging her body to submit to the unrelenting abdominal pressure. Tears streamed down her cheeks as the agony battered her. She just wanted it to end.

Like a cracked dam with a powerful river piling up behind it, the expanding bubble in her gut burst, releasing a torrent of projectile vomit. She threw up again and again until every ounce of food was purged from her body.

As she wiped chunks off her face, she looked down into the toilet bowl. Mixed with chunks of food and blood were swirls of purple mucous.

From the deep and dark recesses of her mind, strange voices reached out across the void and flooded her consciousness with thoughts beyond all human comprehension — thoughts that could annihilate the will, leaving nothing but madness in their wake.

Veronica screamed.

ABOUT THE AUTHOR

Sean Patrick Hazlett is a technologist, finance professional, and science fiction, fantasy, horror, and non-fiction author and editor working in Silicon Valley. He is a winner of the Writers of the Future Contest, and over forty of his short stories have appeared in publications such as *The Year's Best Military and Adventure SF*, *Year's Best Hardcore Horror*, *Robosoldiers*, *Terraform*, *Galaxy's Edge*, *Writers of the Future*, *Grimdark Magazine*, *Vastarien*, and *Abyss & Apex*, among others. He is also the *Weird World War III* and *Weird World War IV* anthologies. Sean is an active member of the Horror Writers Association.

In graduate school, Sean assisted future Secretary of Defense Ashton B. Carter at the Harvard-Stanford Preventive Defense Project where he developed strategic options for confronting Iran's nuclear program. For this analysis, he won the 2006 Policy Analysis Exercise Award at the Harvard Kennedy School of Government. Sean also worked as an intelligence analyst focusing on strategic war games and simulations for the Pentagon, where he drew on his experience training the US military as a cavalry officer in the US Army during the Iraq and Afghan wars.

Sean holds a Master of Business Administration from Harvard Business School, a Master in Public Policy from the Harvard Kennedy School of Government, and bachelor's degrees in History and Electrical Engineering from Stanford University.

artist's rendition of the Lone Pine Mountain Devil

THE LONE PINE
MOUNTAIN DEVIL

(Also known as California
Mountain Devil, or just
Mountain Devil.)

ORIGINS: Simply put, by all accounts these creatures originate from Hell. Where they have been sighted, however, is the Sierra Nevada mountain range, in the American Southwest and Northern Mexico. In particular, as the name dictates, around Lone Pine, California and the Alabama Hills region, in the Inyo national forest.

DESCRIPTION: The LPM Devil is describe as a large bat- or raptor-like creature, furred, with more than one set of wings and sharp talons. Their bite was said to be venomous, with multiple layers of fangs.

By some accounts, their wing-span is in the range of ten feet, with no mention of height.

LIFE CYCLE: Unknown.

HISTORY: tales of the Lone Pine Mountain Devil are cited from the mid- to late 19th century, and even into the early 20th,

both among miners and settlers, and the native population, though no written accounts survive, and no photographs or physical remains are known to exist.

The grimmest account is from around 1878. A group of Spanish settlers — thirty-seven men, women, and children — vanished one night on the trail. They had stopped for a celebration that had gotten out of hand until they were indulging in sinful acts, lighting nearby trees on fire for light and warmth so they could continue into the night. A priest traveling among them disapproved. Father Justus Martinez separated himself from the party. When he heard frightening sounds, he watched in horror from his tent, spared as the Devils attacked and carried the offenders away.

The settlers vanished until two months later when miners discovered their rotting bodies. The priest wandered alone through the wilderness until he arrived at the Mission San Gabriel Arcangel, with nothing but his clothes and a journal detailing that hellish night.

There were other similar accounts from the region with

claims of whole traveling parties found with their faces and chests shredded or eaten to the bone, and the rest of their bodies left untouched. These claims continued all the way up to 1928, but after that there was little mention until 2003, when reported sightings of the creatures recommenced, but no discoveries of gristly remains.

Some believe that these creatures are guardians or protective spirits, attacking only those who destroy nature or disturb the peace of the wilderness, as several key factors in the stories told involved such behavior.

VARIATIONS: It is believed by some that the Lone Pine Mountain Devil is related to the Jersey Devil.

About the Artist

Although Jason Whitley has worn many creative hats, he is at heart a traditional illustrator and painter. With author James Chambers, Jason collaborates and illustrates the sometimes-prose, sometimes graphic novel, *The Midnight Hour,* which is being collected into one volume by eSpec Books. His and Scott Eckelaert's newspaper comic strip, Sea Urchins, has been collected into four volumes. Along with eSpec Books' Systema Paradoxa series, Jason is working on a crime noir graphic novel. His portrait of Charlotte Hawkins Brown is on display in the Charlotte Hawkins Brown Museum.

CAPTURE THE CRYPTIDS!

Cryptid Crate is a monthly subscription box filled with various cryptozoology and paranormal themed items to wear, display and collect. Expect a carefully curated box filled with creeptastic pieces from indie makers and artisans pertaining to bigfoot, sasquatch, UFOs, ghosts, and other cryptid and mysterious creatures (apparel, decor, media, etc).

http://CryptidCrate.com